Solitary Pleasures

stories

Tsipi Keller

Cover and interior design: David Ter-Avanesyan/Ter33Design LLC
Cover art by Odilon Redon (1840-1916), public domain

Some of the stories in this collection originally appeared in
the following publications: *Grey Sparrow Journal, 34thParallel,
Zeek, Elimae, Big Bridge, Wreckage of Reason—
An Anthology of Short Fictions/Spuyten Duyvil,
Unlikely Stories, das gefrorene meer, Scrisul Românesc* (Bucharest),
Quick Fiction, Anthology: *New York Sex* (Painted Leaf Press).

This is a first paperback edition.
Manufactured in the United States

ISBN: 979-8-9917990-0-3 (paperback)

CONTENTS

SOLITARY PLEASURES

The woman in the black & white photograph was leaning forward, smiling, as if offering to the camera, or the photographer, the whole of who she was, the whole of who she thought she was, or wanted you to think she was. She seemed open, friendly, like someone who wouldn't think of hiding anything from you, someone, in fact, who had nothing to hide. And yet, something in her posture, in her shoulders—slanted in a diagonal—suggested to the female viewer that the stranger in the photograph was very much like her: coquettish, apologetic, and with something to hide. Apologetic in the sense of aware, aware that she was posing and putting on her best face, while thoughts of concealment ran through her head. All women, the viewer believed, had something to hide. Most men, she equally believed, were often too impetuous and forward-looking to bother.

Of course, she could be wrong about this. By nature, she was inclined to generalize, but was also willing to admit that her views, in general, were possibly skewed.

This was the dilemma of women who thought too much, the viewer thought. Her name was Eve, the mother of all females and, come to think of it, of all males, too, but males, for the most part, forgot, or did their best to forget, that they came from Eve. The Bible confirmed their instincts, stressing the import of loins rather than wombs, as in: "... and kings shall come out of thy loins." In those golden olden days, a man needed do nothing more than place his hand on his muscular right thigh when making a vow.

As a child, beginning to grasp the adult world and its dissimulations, Eve was titillated when encountering "loins" in Bible class. She sensed the supremacy in the word, its sexual potency, and while the instructor, a gaunt, gentle man with thin, pale hands and a tangled red beard, belabored the holiness of the text, she gave herself over to the odd and wondrous sensations that began in her mind and traveled down her spine, stirring her small and healthy vagina. A vague sense of shame—and yes, concealment—also stirred in her, but not as powerfully.

There was a lot to be confused about while growing up, and Eve, intelligent without knowing herself to be intelligent, accepted this state of confusion with equanimity. She looked up to the adults around her, she obeyed them, but more as a strategy than true belief and conviction. In the tender tissues of her evolving personality, she felt sorry for them, which made it easier to deceive them. What you don't know can't hurt you, she heard them say again and again, and she took it to heart.

This was how children do not learn from the mistakes of their elders, Eve thought. She put away the magazine with the smiling woman in it, and consulted the small digital clock on the bedside table. Seven o'clock. In the morning. It was Sunday, and her Sunday routine demanded only that she get the paper and have coffee in the small bakery-café on the avenue. Christmas was done and over with and, next week, New Year's and its upbeat hysteria was to be upon them, after which the creaky rotation of week after week would resume, and the new year would be new no longer.

There was no cat or dog she needed to feed or to walk, and yet she rose early, if with difficulty. She loved sleep, but also wished to be awake for as many hours as was humanly practical. She wasn't an optimist, but being awake and active gave her the illusion of hope, of things yet to come. She lived in the apartment her grandparents, Leon and Sarah, had lived and died in, a two-bedroom co-op in the East Thirties, and, working part-time for a travel agency, she made enough to subsist. When she needed something extra, like paying her dentist for a cleaning, she dug into her grandparents' savings. She had a degree in Comparative Literature, which Leon and Sarah had paid for, and just when it was time for her to prove herself and make them proud, Sarah got sick, and then Leon, as if in sympathy, also got sick, and she moved back in with them to nurse and watch them die. It was her first fulltime job, filling out the medical forms, talking to the doctors, taking the one, then the other, to the various clinics and hospitals for tests and treatments. Not to mention shopping, cooking, cleaning. At twenty-eight, she mused, she had become the mother of her grandparents, instilling a sense of urgency in the doctors and nurses to do all they could, just as Leon and Sarah had done for her when she was sick and under their care.

The elderly neighbors praised her, her devotion, so rare these days, children are born ungrateful, and so on. "It's the European way," they murmured, meaning that Eve's grandparents, being Europeans, had given Eve a European education.

No!—her brain offered a muted reply, while she nodded and smiled politely as the situation demanded. They had given a European education, if that's what it was, to my mother as well, and she turned out to be wild and unmanageable, and the complications she died of had to do with drugs, so there!

But, of course, she never disabused the kind, elderly neighbors, they were a family of sorts, and often borrowed her "young" eyes to thread a needle, or to read the small print of documents. So, she let them stop her on the street, in the hallways, in the mailroom, and watched as they shook their heads sorrowfully and asked if there was something they could do to help. She always said, No, all is under control, actually embarrassed by their offers. Why she was embarrassed she wasn't sure and hadn't had the time to ponder, but now, seven months after Sarah's passing, and four months after Leon's, she concluded she must have sensed or understood that Leon and Sarah, shamed by their illness, and knowing that the end was near, had wanted no one but her.

Working for the travel agency was soothing. The people who came to see her, or called on the telephone, were a happy, carefree bunch, booking a flight, a package deal, the ideal vacation. It was around the corner from her home, and Sybil, the woman she worked for, had known her grandparents, was aware of Eve's sacrifice, and was therefore civil in a way she might not have been under the normal circumstance of employer / employee.

And yet, both women knew that one day soon, Eve would have to leave and start pursuing a real career. With a degree in Comparative Literature her options were limited, and therefore wide open. She would have to specialize in something, although she wasn't yet sure what form that specialization would take. Before Leon and Sarah got sick, she considered going for her PhD and then teaching in some university, but those plans were scratched, perhaps for good. Now that she no longer had to prove herself, nothing seemed that important, or terribly pressing. Sybil, an attractive brunette who favored mini dresses, high heels, and false eyelashes, said that Eve should take her time and not push herself too hard; after all, she was still in shock, she was still mourning, and she wasn't even thirty, so what's the hurry? And Eve had to agree: Yes, she was still in shock, she was still mourning, and not even thirty.

Still, she did have to contend with the reality that she lived in a heady age of accelerated expectations; everyone around her, young and old, seemed to be rushing somewhere, purposefully. All her friends had already established their place in life, or, at least, knew where they were headed. And, Sybil herself, was not only a mother of three grown children, which was an achievement in itself, but also the founder and president of her own successful business.

Some women just had the knack for it, for all of it. They had strong, sure voices. There was never as much as a quaver of hesitation in Sybil's voice, and Eve wondered if Sybil ever stopped to question herself, if she ever had a moment of doubt, or if everything indeed was so clear in her mind. She liked to imagine Sybil's bathroom countertops, the abundance of expensive brushes and combs and creams and colognes. She liked the way Sybil let her heels drag a little across the floor, generating a captivating echoing sound, a kind of ricochet that, Eve imagined, accompanied and enhanced Sybil's sense of importance and nonchalance.

Eve found Sybil, and women like Sybil, sexy, if in a slightly vulgar way. She had held the vague notion that such women always married men who were aggressive and assertive like them, but Lucas, Sybil's husband, was gentle and soft-spoken, and seemed to be in awe of Sybil. He wasn't handsome in the conventional sense, but he was slender, about six feet tall, and stooping a little—aristocratically, Eve thought— his blondish, graying hair cropped short above his pale, high forehead. Once, when Eve caught him looking at Sybil with a hidden smile on his face, a smile that suggested wonder and admiration for his wife who was out there, engaged and thriving in the chaos of people's unpre- dictable ways, Eve became aware that she liked him, from a distance. She liked his kindness, which she perceived as the core and at the root of his intelligence. It was during one of his visits to Travel Light, and he stood at the door to Sybil's office, like a supplicant, waiting for her to get off the phone. Sybil had acknowledged him with a wave of her hand, but continued her conversation, sounding more effusive than usual, possibly because of his presence. Then Sybil got off the phone and, standing up, pulled down her tight-fitting dress, wiggling her hips and smiling at Lucas with pure, child-like delight. He went to her and they exchanged a quick kiss, murmuring a few words, then Lucas helped Sybil into her coat and the two of them left for lunch, and Eve thought how romantic it was that a husband and wife, married for so many years, went out to lunch together.

He was some kind of writer, Eve knew. Philosophical stuff, Sybil had said, and Eve asked—out of politeness, but curiosity as well—if she could read something of his, and Sybil said that Lucas was very private about his work and showed it only to a very select group of friends. "Doesn't he want to publish?" Eve had asked, and Sybil said yes, but not during his lifetime. "Posthumously, you mean?" Eve said, and Sybil gave her a look the meaning of which Eve could not decipher, before replying with a shrug, "I guess so."

One day—Eve thought bravely—I will be like Sybil. No longer a girl, but a hundred percent woman, fully formed. I will have life experiences, maybe a business, a husband, even kids of my own. I won't be timid or passive about it. I'll work toward it after this period of mourning and adjusting is over and done with.

She wasn't a mourner by nature, she didn't think. She didn't feel as though she were actively mourning her grandparents, but she accepted it as a possibility, if only because she was feeling sort of numb these past few months. Of course, it wasn't necessarily their deaths that made her feel numb, it could be her own life, her own future, her own uncertainty. But, it was also true that when Leon and Sarah were living, it was easier for her to focus on plans for the future. Perhaps it was their immigrant story that had focused her, their steadfast optimistic outlook, their Yiddish, their broken English, the fact that, from an early age, she had been their mouth and ears. Until age five or so, Eve, too, spoke Yiddish, but, as she acquired the English she lost the Yiddish, even though Leon had tried to keep it alive in their home, battling Sarah who had insisted they speak English. At the time Eve didn't give it much thought, she was actually happy and eager to forget the immigrant Yiddish, but now regretted that she let herself lose that juicy tongue in her mouth.

They, Leon and Sarah, were not remarkable in any obvious way. Two people, uprooted, dislocated, survivors of the vilest premeditated calamity in history. A chance meeting in a store, a marriage, a life resumed with apprehension, but resumed all the same. A baby, a beautiful firstborn daughter, hope personified, and then a calamity, nearly as traumatic, or perhaps even more traumatic than the earlier one, the beautiful firstborn, a daughter, Rivkale, personifying hope, died of pneumonia. Five years later another daughter came, Ruth, who, unmarried and rebellious, had given birth to Eve and died shortly after of complications.

Complications—Eve's stomach contracted in a knot. Her life was a complicated muddle before it even began, and every time she thought about the people missing from her life—a potential mother, a potential aunt, an unknown father—her stomach knotted. You would think that with the years the hurt would diminish, but it didn't. She couldn't even begin to fathom how Leon and Sarah had withstood all their losses, how they continued to live. In a way, it was nearly inhuman, or maybe noble—she couldn't or wouldn't decide.

Outside her window snow was falling, soft and ethereal. She felt romantic, a state she lapsed into when she came to an impasse; it was easy, comforting, and it seduced her. Women, she had read, were, by nature, prone to idle romantic musing. So be it. Her brain was a mass of flitting thoughts, flitting but durable enough to bring about conflicting insights and emotions.

An hour later, sitting in the bakery, she read the paper and slowly sipped the strong and hot coffee, greedily devouring a buttered poppy seed roll. Poppy and sesame seeds were a favorite with Leon and Sarah, and with her as well. Jews, Leon liked to joke, were fond consumers of seeds, from time immemorial seeking to strike roots. Jews, even before they signed an exclusivity pact with God, were a marginal, persecuted tribe of undesirables, poor and living off the land. "Must be something in our genes, we're always the foreigner. Thank God for Israel," Leon would conclude, and Sarah and Eve would accept it as fact.

She became aware of the guy behind the counter, who began humming a tune, and she wondered if he was humming to get her attention, or was totally oblivious of her; once he had served her coffee, he forgot she was there. She knew him by sight and, she guessed, he probably knew her, she came here nearly every weekend, but he never let on that he recognized her. He was young, in his thirties, and she thought he might be the owner, or the owner's son; he had the caring, responsible air of a proprietor. At this early hour, she was the only customer and, once in a while, she raised her head from the paper and gazed out the floor-to-ceiling window, as if to remind herself of where she was. A light but persistent drizzle was falling, and except for an occasional passing car, and a couple of men walking their dogs, the street was deserted. There was no trace of the snow that had fallen earlier—had she dreamt it?

"How was your Christmas?"

"Oh, good." She looked up, blushing a little, surprised that he finally addressed her when he didn't have to. "How was yours?"

"Thank God it's over, that's all I can say." He cackled as he cleaned the counter with a dishrag, as if suddenly discomfited for having spoken.

"Yeah," Eve said, attempting a cackle of her own, but it came out wrong, more like a croak. "Was it snowing earlier?" She added, as cover-up.

"I don't know, I was inside." He gestured toward the back.

"Oh." She nodded, with intent, since she couldn't think what else to say. She noted the tattoos on his forearms, which reminded her of Leon and Sarah, as tattooed arms usually did. She was about six or seven years old when she first noticed the blue crooked numbers on their arms and asked what they were and how they had gotten them, and they told her. Did it hurt? She asked, and they said they couldn't remember anymore, but that yes, it probably hurt. Later on, when she understood that the Nazis had done this to them and to many other Jews, she tried to imagine how long it took them to tattoo so many people, so many arms.

"It's supposed to snow later," the guy behind the counter said.

"Yes." She nodded. There were a couple of tables outside under the awning, and she considered moving there, but worried that he might think she was moving outside because she didn't want to talk to him.

"You know," she said, "I think I'll try sitting outside, get some fresh air?"

"Sure, why not, it's not too cold."

Once outside, she took out her diary and pen and wrote down the date and hour. Across the street, where a line of thin bare trees marked the median strip, a man stood under his umbrella, waiting for his dog to finish its business. When the dog was done, the man pulled a plastic bag from his pocket and bent down, trying to keep his umbrella steady while holding onto the leashed golden retriever. It was interesting, Eve thought, how most people, herself included, would flinch and balk at picking up the excrement of another human being, but thought nothing of cleaning up after a dog. Once, talking to her friend Diana—the proud owner of two Chihuahuas—Eve said that she had thought of a new, money-making venture, a home for the aged dog, and Diana said dog owners would never put their dog in a home. "Why not?" Eve asked. "Because dog owners love their dogs." Diana had emphasized "love," perhaps to imply that Eve would know nothing about such love since Eve didn't have a dog. "But they put their parents in a home," Eve said. "That's true." Diana laughed her charming, helpless laugh. "Makes you wonder, doesn't it?"

Looking down at the white page, Eve thought she might write about the guy behind the counter finally talking to her, just mention him in passing as she had done a few weekends ago when she heard him talk to a man, perhaps a regular customer like herself. She liked his voice and what he said, something about his cat coughing up his carpet in small balls of hair. But, if he never spoke to her again, why give him an importance he didn't deserve? She was new at this diary writing business, and was still unsure what she wanted it to be. She told herself that she could and should allow herself more spontaneity, but hadn't gotten to that stage yet. She bought the notebook a few weeks into Sarah's and Leon's ailments, intending it to be a ledger where she would record what the doctors had said. But then, almost imperceptibly, her thoughts and feelings began to filter in, and she found that it comforted her, writing down her worries, her hopes, her frustrations.

She waited for another concrete thought. The rain had intensified, playing its steady splattering music on the pavement. Everything turned gray, nearly dark, even the occasional passing car was gray, but, as she sat and watched the rain, translucently white against the gray, a sudden feeling washed over her, a feeling of wholeness, a sudden elation, as if, for a moment, her spirit, her soul, had taken over. As if, for a moment, something elemental had taken over, obliterating everyday concerns and worries, obliterating selfhood and ego, allowing her the brief but heightened recognition that even for this moment, of sitting and watching the rain, holding a cup of coffee in her hand and feeling the cold breeze on her cheeks, life was worth living.

The man had finished cleaning after his dog and dumped the plastic bag in the trashcan. He then stood a moment and contemplated the street before pulling on the leash and going back the way he came; home, Eve supposed. Toward the end, when Leon was transferred to a hospice, when his mind, in spurts of lucidity, was still there, when Eve, not a hundred percent sure that he knew who she was, when a nurse had failed to come quickly enough to his bed after he had shat, the girl Eve, unable to bear the thought that her grandfather was lying in his own excrement, pulled down the pants of his pajamas, then his underwear, and began to wipe away the brownish liquid, raising his balls and penis, the involuntary realization crossing her mind that that was where her mother had originated, from these balls, shrunken and withered, from this penis that had given her grandmother pleasure, and she looked up from her task, briefly, and saw Leon's fierce brown eyes watching her with the confused recognition that someone, a female, was touching his private parts, recognizing perhaps that it was she, Eve, his granddaughter, touching him where it was forbidden, but also perhaps grasping that it was necessary, that he had just shat and someone was cleaning him, someone familiar, perhaps his granddaughter, perhaps his daughter, and then the nurse arrived and admonished, gently, "You shouldn't be doing this," as she pulled the privacy curtain around the bed and told Eve to go and wash her hands.

Taking a deep breath, Eve raised her head and looked up at the sky, trying to un-trigger the threatening tears. Not even one little cloud in the gray mass, she thought. One little cloud to focus on.

"Hello there, mind if I join you?" The counter guy materialized before her, startling her, a huge Mickey Mouse coffee mug in his hand. He had put on a leather jacket over his white apron and t-shirt, but didn't bother to zip it up.

"Sorry I startled you." He pulled a chair and sat down, smiling at her, and she smiled back, recovering, shutting the notebook and putting her hands in her lap, just in case they began to shake. "Interesting," he continued, "that we're so easily shaken. Must be an instinctual remnant from our past."

"Yeah." Eve nodded, clearing her throat.

"Are you okay?"

"Mickey Mouse," she said, pointing at his cup. He had strong hands, she noted, and wore no rings.

"Indeed. A birthday gift from my nephew. You a writer?" He motioned the notebook with a subtle chin movement.

"No, it's just . . ." She waved her hand, not intending to complete the sentence. She hadn't actually given him permission to join her, and yet, here he was, obviously assuming, or pretending to assume, she wanted his company.

"Many writers in the neighborhood, you know. They're all my customers. We have a cool thing going on here."

"Cool—how?"

"Oh, just talking and stuff. They let me read their stories, they think I'm a good judge, like, a good reader or something, a regular guy sort of thing."

"Are you?" she asked. "A regular guy?"

"Sort of. We all are, aren't we, regular guys, except for those moments when we aren't?"

"Hmm." Eve nodded thoughtfully as if deeply absorbed in what he had just said. It was quite banal, actually, but, for now, she was willing to give him the benefit of doubt and listen to what else he had to say. He had a promising physique, the kind of male physique that conjured images of comfort and security in certain female minds, her mind. Ah, to lay her head and rest a while. She wondered if he had a smooth or hairy chest.

A man and a woman hurried past their table and entered the bakery, the man holding the door for the woman and glancing at them before going in. He looked familiar, though Eve couldn't place him.

"Don't you have to—?" She gestured toward the café.

"No, my brother's inside. The father of my nephew."

"Oh." She laughed, suddenly feeling light and oddly happy.

"We're partners. He's the money man, I'm the baker."

"A baker." She took time to digest. "I've never met a baker before."

"There are quite a few of us around."

"I'm sure. Do you mind if I smoke?"

"No, go ahead."

She offered him a cigarette, which he shook off with a hint of reproach in his eyes. Please, not a health freak, she thought and lit one, blowing the smoke away from him.

"Kent," he said. "Kind of old-fashioned."

She smiled. "My grandma used to smoke them, so I smoke them too. They're a kind of bridge, connecting me to her."

"You were close?"

"Yes, very."

"Well, I'm sure she'd rather you didn't smoke at all. Cigarettes are bad for you, you know."

"I know." She pursed her lips. "I don't smoke much, and I do plan to quit at some point."

He nodded and looked out to the street, so she did, too. The drizzle had stopped, and there was more traffic on the road. She tried to think of something interesting to say, something that would capture their imaginations and get them going, but nothing came. It never did when she needed it most.

"So," he said after a while.

"So," she echoed.

"How are we doing?"

"All right, I think," she said, hating her frozen passivity.

"I've been watching you for these past few weeks. You strike me as someone whose pleasures are solitary."

Wow, she thought, looking at him. Her mind flashed on "been watching you," then dwelled on "solitary" and "pleasures" as she tried to determine if he was aware of what he was insinuating, or if the words simply flew out of his mouth before he had time to rethink their double-entendre. His face was square and hard, but his eyes were deep brown, like Leon's, and heavy-lidded, also like Leon's. A friend once told her that heavy lids were a sign of a strong libido. She asked herself if this was his way of flirting with her, and if she might want to encourage him.

"You're very direct," she finally said, slowly and deliberately. "Maybe a touch too direct?" She smiled to show him she didn't mean to criticize, just stating a fact. "Maybe that's your way of taking control of a situation?"

"What situation?"

"Whatever situation you find yourself in, or initiate."

"Could be." His face revealed nothing. She couldn't tell if he agreed with her, or had taken offense. Her usual impulse was to retreat, to say something cheery and mollifying, but this morning she went against it, keeping quiet, waiting for him to say more.

"I'm Aaron," he said, extending his hand.

"Eve." She put her hand in his. His was large and warm, hers was small and cold. She wondered if he was Jewish.

"Eve," he said, "I like Eve, I don't know anyone named Eve."

"I like Aaron," she reciprocated. "I don't know anyone named Aaron, although"—She paused a moment. Leon's younger brother,

Aaron, had perished in the camps. And, it came to her in a flash, on Rosh Hashanah and Yom Kippur, coming home from synagogue, Leon would place his large hand on her head, reciting the blessing of Moses and Aaron, a blessing normally reserved for boys. This past Yom Kippur had been the first she had spent without Leon and Sarah, and on the eve of Yom Kippur she lit Yahrzeit candles for them, saying a short and improvised prayer, asking God to guard and bless their souls, and the next morning, in synagogue for the Yizkor service, she was terribly embarrassed and self-conscious when she had to rise with those who had lost a family member during the past year, while the rest of the congregation remained seated, watching her, she felt, with a thousand pitying eyes.

"We did have an Aaron in the family."

"What happened to him?"

"He died," she said in as neutral a tone as she could summon. She looked into her cup—it was empty. "I like Aaron. It's primal. Biblical."

"And you wonder if I'm a Jew or a Lutheran." He threw his head back and laughed, and she, amused, observed his smooth and strong throat, glad to note that his Adam's apple didn't show.

"Not at all." She gave him a wry look. His mouth, too, was just right, his lips not too thick and not too thin, and his teeth were clean and even. "But, since you brought it up, which is it?"

"Neither."

She nodded, hiding her disappointment.

"I know who Eve was, but who was Aaron?" he asked.

"Moses' brother."

"Moses, hmmm, I didn't know that. Was he a good man?"

"Oh, yes, a very good man, actually." She came alive. "He was a man of peace. Legend has it that he hated arguments, and always made peace between rivals, even if he had to deceive them both to achieve it. I like to think of him as my model."

"Really." He rubbed his cheek, calling her attention to his pale skin

—he had shaved this morning, and possibly every morning. "Why did he have to deceive them?"

"It was his strategy. He would go to X and say, Y really wants to make peace with you, but doesn't know how. Then he would go to Y and say the same about X, and then X and Y would fall into each other's arms, friends forever." She laughed, uneasily, thinking that she was boring him.

"How come you know so much about the Bible?" he asked.

"My grandparents. They wanted me to have a traditional Jewish education, so they sent me to Hebrew school."

"Interesting." He drank the last of his coffee. "Ready for a refill? On the house."

She nodded, smiling a small, impish smile, feeling warm and cozy inside, as if he had offered to protect her, to take her under the proverbial male wing.

He went in, and she put away her diary and pen. What now, she wondered. She was sitting with her back to the café and itched to turn around and look inside, get a better look at the brother and watch Aaron as he poured her coffee. Maybe pouring his heart into it as well, she mused further, wallowing in her own silliness. How eager, how easily seduced.

"I only have a minute." Aaron reappeared, putting her coffee before her. She was now among the privileged, steaming coffee in a yellow mug rather than a Styrofoam cup. "My brother needs me inside, but I wanted to ask you . . ."

Eve looked up at him. He remained standing, and didn't have his coffee with him. "What?" She asked, knowing what was coming, she was used to it.

"Why is it, you know, your grandparents. Why were they in charge of your education?"

Eve licked her lips and made a matter-of-fact smacking sound. "Well, they raised me. My mother died when I was very young, and my father, well, we don't know who my father was. Is."

As she spoke, she could see his brain clicking a check mark in the fitting box: not an orphan exactly, but an orphan all the same.

"You're kidding," he said slowly, then stuck his hands in the pockets of his apron and leaned forward on his toes. "I mean, no, of course you're not kidding. It's, well, amazing to me, but not to you, I don't think."

"No, it's amazing to me, too."

"You'll have to tell me the rest of it some time. Come and see us more often, all right?" He gave her a broad smile, and she responded with a vague, confused one as he turned and strode back inside.

Solitary pleasures, indeed! Eve thought. So, not quite an auspicious beginning, and maybe not a beginning at all, just a friendly chat with a regular customer. No matter. She had a fresh cup of coffee before her, and the morning still felt crisp and new. Maybe it would have been better if he had continued to ignore her, so she could continue to come here, solitary and anonymous. And yet, maybe not. Maybe it was good that he spoke to her. Maybe it was good to look forward to something, keeping in mind that assuming too much or expecting too much wouldn't be wise.

THE HORSE

Jaffa, 1954

MY FATHER leads us up the hill. It is Saturday, a day off for the Jews, and my father's horse is with us.

This horse and my father work hard all week and on Saturdays they go for a walk, with me and my sister and our friends tagging along. We are serious children, though we do not know it. We are serious and determined because we are new to our parents, and our parents are new to the landscape and climate. But my sister, I think, is too serious; she is a year younger than me, and she hardly ever smiles or talks, she only listens.

It is bare and dusty up the dirt road, and the prevalent color is the color of ash. Small stones fly into our sandals and land between our toes, but we do not stop. We shake our feet and continue, watching how our sandals and skin change color where the dust settles.

We are a sight. First is this man, my father, tall and muscular, his skin rough and brown from the sun. Then there is this horse, also brown, and then nine or ten children marching behind. My father is in charge of the horse, and I am in charge of the children. We are five or six years old, but because the horse belongs to my father, they concede leadership to me, his eldest daughter.

Busy climbing, we are silent, but not unhappy. We all live in the same house on the main street of a neighborhood called The Great Zone.

During the day we are allowed to go beyond the gate of our courtyard, but not too far. During the night our parents lock the gate and we are not allowed to go out because at night the bad people come. They do bad things, especially the women whom all the parents call kurvë, when they sit and talk in the courtyard and forget that we are there. Kurvë are bad because kurvë do bad things with their bodies for money. Even our parents don't go out at night, except on Friday night when the men have to go to the synagogue to pray.

During the day it is very exciting on our street, and very noisy. There are merchants and street vendors, and all sorts of Arabs and Jews, and carts pulled by horses, and carts pulled by donkeys, and the porous smell of manure is everywhere. The horses neigh, impatiently stomping their front hooves, but the donkeys, as ever, seem resigned to their fate. They remind me of my sister, they have the same long ears and the same quiet, downcast look in their dark brown eyes. My sister's ears, in fact, are the joke of the family.

The Arabs wear their long white robes and they tie keffiyehs around their heads. They are loud, they shout and yell in Arabic, waving their arms. The Jews, like my father, wear shirts and pants, short or long, depending if it's hot or cold. The Jews are also loud, they yell in Yiddish and other languages, like Romanian and Hungarian and Polish. My parents and our neighbors speak all the languages, but life for the adults, I am thinking, is hot and hectic, and they seem to burn with their troubles.

Once in a while, strange children come to our street. When my friends and I come face to face with a group of them, the air intensifies and there is great defiance on both sides, and hostility. They are the Israeli ones, they speak Hebrew, and we know they mock us from the way they point at us and laugh, ridiculing our clothes and our Yiddish. There is not much we can do to stop them. We look them up and down, but our lips remain tight. They may be older than us, but in our eyes they are nothing but hoodlums. The truth is, they scare us. They look alien and aloof in their khaki shorts and shirts: they are the enemy, they were born here, they are called Sabra. We and our parents are newcomers. We came from Europa, and we are called Olim Hadashim in that Hebrew language.

Life is exciting and chaotic on our street, but as soon as we step through the gate inside our walled-in courtyard, it is safe and quiet. We live in an old stone house that was once an Arab school, before we and our neighbors moved in. It is a long, one-story building that was converted by the Jewish Agency into one-room flats for new immigrants like us. A corridor connects all the flats, about ten of them, and this is where we play when it rains, with the doors to the flats open. But most of the time it is hot and dry, and we play in the courtyard, or run around on the street. My father says our family is lucky because our flat is at the end of the corridor, and our window faces the sea, which is right below us, down the hill. The salt of the sea is good for us, my father says. Everything is either good or bad for us, and my father and mother will tell us which is which. My sister and I listen to every word they say because they are our parents and we love them. Both of them have a blue tattoo on their forearms: it is a series of wobbly, crooked numbers, amateurishly carved under the skin. It is a number they got from the Nazis, and I ask them if it hurt when the Nazis did this to them. They say, yes, it hurt, it hurt very much, and they tell me more about the Nazis and what they did, and how God finally punished them. When my parents and our neighbors mention the Nazis, they spit on the ground and curse *yimach shmam v'zichram.*

Our family is small and brand new. It is just my father, my mother, my sister and I, and we all sleep in the one room with the window that faces the sea. The horse sleeps outside, tied to a tree near our window. Except for our neighbors, no one comes to see us, but one night we did have a guest who came from afar to visit us. He was my father's cousin, he lived in a kibbutz, and he had come to town on some kibbutz business. He arrived late, I had already been put to bed, but when he bent down to have a look at me, how dark and handsome his face looked in the moonlight! How beautiful his smile! How I fluttered with joy all over and fell in love maybe for the first time.

We reach the top of the hill and now it is flat land and we can relax our pace. Everybody senses this, even the horse, and soon the single file breaks up, and we walk in a dense, large group, my father and the horse slightly ahead of us. We can talk now, discuss whatever it is we need to discuss. I am thinking about what my father told me the night before: beginning tomorrow, Sunday evening, the horse will be moving to a stable where he will be more comfortable. When my father tells me this, I, of course, am against it. I ask him if it will cost us money. My father laughs; it amuses him no end that I worry about money.

But, everything costs money, and we do not have much. Yet, there is always enough for me and my sister to run out through the gate with a coin in one sweaty palm and a glass in the other, and buy sahlab from the Arab vendor who comes around with his donkey and cart. The sahlab is white and thick and hot, and even my father and mother like it. It smells sweet, and it is sweet, and my father says it is good for us: it is made with milk and corn flour. The Arab fills our glasses from a spigot, sprinkles cinnamon and grated coconut on top, and we mix it with a spoon and eat it, right there on the street.

Another prominent Arab on our street is Derby, and sometimes my father borrows the name when he wants to play "crazy" to amuse us. Derby wears a long white robe and is the exclusive and certified "loony" on our street. He talks to himself, shouts and gestures, and hurls stones at us when we manage to get his attention. I do not know where our parents are when we do such things; the stones could be dangerous, our street is dangerous.

My mother, like my sister, does not say much, she is quiet. But with the other women in the house she talks and laughs and blushes a lot. I think she is the youngest, or, at least, the prettiest. She is slim, and she wears nice clothes my father bought for her when they lived in

Prague, before they came here and brought me with them. Some of my mother's dresses have her initials embroidered on the left side under the collarbone, and I pray that one day she will let me wear them. My mother has a beautiful voice and she likes to sing sad Yiddish songs her mother used to sing, telling us that sorrow is a gift, that sorrow helps people to find one another.

There are all sorts of Jews, but the Jews we live with are good Jews: they are our neighbors, and they, too, came from Europa where it was not so hot, and where big fat trees grew out of the snow, and where every morning my father bundled me up and put me in my carriage and took me for a walk until the Communists came. Then we came here and my sister was born, which, my mother says, was an accident.

Now we walk with the horse along the dirt road, and I watch the muscles of his behind bounce from side to side. I know that horses do not have to stop when they have to pooh: they just keep on walking and the stuff pours out of them, steaming hot and yellow, like mashed straw. We are used to the smell because Jaffa has many horses, and our horse sometimes goes in the yard. Our neighbors do not mind it even though the courtyard is our shared living room and bathroom and sometimes kitchen. Every morning the mothers bring out round tin pails and, with a long hose, fill them with water. The sun heats up the water, and we the children plunge in for our daily bath, while our mothers stand under the trees, their arms bare and pink. They tell each other stories and laugh. All the other mothers are kind of big and their hair is pulled back under a kerchief.

In the afternoon we come out again with small tables and chairs and fruits and nuts. Our mothers drink tea and talk some more, while we the kids chase each other, or tease the ants out of their holes. Then the fathers come home from work, and my mother and my sister and I go to the gate to welcome my father and the horse. My mother brings with her a glass of tea and we stand and watch my father drink it, while my mother tells him all that has happened during the day.

While we walk, I suddenly notice that my father no longer holds onto the rope tied to the horse's neck. Instead, he has allowed himself to linger behind the horse and join us, the children. Instantly anxious, I warn him: "The horse will run away!" I wag my finger at him, as my mother sometimes does, but he does not listen. He laughs and tells me not to worry, the horse will not run away.

I know that he loves to listen to children as they twist their tongues in Yiddish. Still, I tell him again to go back to his horse, and again he laughs. There is nothing I can do but watch the horse and wait for him to take off.

And then, all at once, he does. He charges ahead and we all freeze and watch him disappear. Then my father calls after him and begins running. I run after my father, calling him. Behind me my sister is running, also calling. We run and run and suddenly there is nothing and no one in sight, not my father, not the horse. Now it is only me and my sister, looking for my father. "I knew it," I tell her. "I knew it."

We arrive at a wide road lined with a few low houses. A group of men and women is seated on the stoop of one of the houses, and they watch us with the mild interest of adults with a few hours of leisure on their hands. They are Jews, I think, those Israeli Jews. I go over to them and ask if they saw a man running after a horse. They are merry, they laugh, they think it's funny. They gesticulate and they talk, but it is Hebrew they are speaking and I can't understand a word. My sister kicks some dirt at them, and I take her by the hand and leave them to their mirth, my eyes filling with tears as I dare repeat the only curse I know, in a language I don't know, *yimach shmam v'zichram*.

In the end, my father did find the horse and the two of them came home together, and we kissed and hugged the horse because we knew that starting tomorrow he would be moving to a stable, and that every evening my father would come home without him, and that he would walk through the gate into the courtyard, which meant that my sister and I and my mother would not be going out to the street to meet my

father and the horse and bring him his tea and watch him drink it while
mother told him everything that had happened during the day.

BAD THOUGHTS

Again she cut herself—quite badly—slicing a tomato at the kitchen counter and thinking bad thoughts. It was the bad thoughts, she thought, as she reached for a paper towel, pressed it against the wound and hurried to the bathroom for a bandaid. As usual when she cut herself, she worried about infection and having to go to hospital to have it looked at, but this time, as all the other times, she didn't go, the wound healed in a day or two, there was no infection, she didn't die, and not even a scar remained. She berated herself for being so:

1. clumsy

2. careless

3. spaced out

and, as punishment, she now had to deal with the blood and struggle with the bandage, not to mention the pain and the shock to her system, in addition to which, with a thumb out of commission, she'd have a hard time flossing her teeth, lighting a cigarette, and yes, slicing a tomato. In short, she'd feel like an invalid until it healed, and all because she was thinking her bad thoughts and wasn't paying attention as one should when handling a sharp knife. She was a loser and a fuck-up, no, she wasn't, others were, and that's why the bad thoughts invaded when they did. Only moments before, before she decided it was time for dinner, she was sitting in her living room, reading Iris Murdoch's *Nuns and Soldiers*, and came across a beautiful passage ("A strong sense of duty, of the cast-iron necessity of decent behavior, was a positive characteristic of both Guy and Gertrude, something which, when you knew them well, was as evident in them as the colour of their hair and eyes"), a passage that described her feelings exactly, and she took a moment to savor the kinship, for she, too, believed that people should try to be decent, act decently, and so it happened that precisely the passage that pleased her so, was also the cause of the bad thoughts, because thinking of the passage while slicing the tomato brought to mind a married couple she knew who were not decent and were therefore the subject of the bad thoughts, and thoughts of revenge also appeared, and that was when the knife sliced into her thumb, nearly cutting off a piece of flesh that, mercifully, wasn't cut all the way and still clung to the rest of her.

APPLIANCES,
A MODERN FAIRY TALE

Life is totally about losing everything.
Mike Tyson

As in every contemporary home, things hummed and beeped in Lily's kitchen, and she, responsive by nature, would murmur, Yes, dear, I know, will get to it in a minute. Every time something beeped in her house, she compared the beep to Jerry, her husband, but not favorably. Too often, she felt, he was abusive, if not physically, then mouthly, if not deliberately, then indifferently. The beeps, on the other hand, were always gentle, non-pressing, just reminders to take this or that out of the oven, the microwave, and each time, without fail, her heart opened with gratitude. And indeed, just beeping machines, but machines that were programmed to care and be on her side.

No, she and Jerry did not have what was commonly considered a bad marriage. Their marriage, Lily knew, wasn't exceptional. From what she saw and heard around her, and occasionally on the news, it was clear that marriage was difficult on all who were involved in it, and that it was never, or only rarely, all peaches and cream. Her mother had told her as much many years ago, but she didn't take it to heart. At the time she thought it was her mother's lot, and now it seemed it was hers as well.

Even though she was only a housewife—a terrible and awful term that sounded as though she were the wife of the house, that she was wifing the house. She had, for the most part, a good opinion of herself, an opinion corroborated by friends and neighbors. She was a decent person, always diligent in her housework, even finding pleasure in it. She wasn't very demanding, her needs didn't run very deep and, more importantly, while dusting and cooking, she was able to listen to music and let her mind wander wherever it pleased.

Also, she was methodical and conscientious, tallying up her day, the things she had accomplished and could cross off her To Do list. She always tried to find something positive to say about the day, so she wouldn't have to conclude it had been a waste. It was a mental process she indulged in, usually toward evening, just before Jerry came home from the office. This is not to say that her day was over when he arrived. There was still dinner to be served and eaten, dishes cleared and carefully placed in the dishwasher, some chit-chat with Jerry, if he was in the mood, and then the TV, and finally, around eleven, the brushing of teeth and climbing onto the high, king-size bed.

At least that, she thought, a king-size bed. It was roomy, it was her salvation, she felt luxurious in it, she had her own down cover and Jerry had his. It didn't make for romantic cuddling in the middle of the night, but it was practical, as Jerry was no longer likely to cuddle her in the middle of the night. He usually fell asleep instantly, and she would lie there, on her back, on the left side of the bed, for another good hour or so, thinking small thoughts, sometimes re-tallying her day and deciding once again that, indeed, she had justified her existence, even if in a small, not very notable measure, and thus earned her sleep. The issue of waste was an obsession with her, all kinds of waste, material and mental. It was a petty obsession, it annoyed her, it made her go to absurd lengths, saving a dishrag, for instance, but no matter how hard she tried to resist it, she always gave in to it. She berated herself for being the type of person who would save a dishrag, but her compulsion to save it was stronger than her exasperation. No one, not even her friends, was aware of this inner conflict and, at times, she worried she might drive herself insane if she didn't find her way out of these clashing forces.

"Good night, sweetheart," Jerry said, startling her, but only briefly, as she quickly realized he had addressed Nancy, the cat he came home with two nights ago. They had never had a pet before, had never discussed having a pet, but, Jerry explained, someone at the office had found the cat on the highway, and Jerry volunteered to give her a home.

It surprised Lily. She hadn't known Jerry to be a cat lover, but she didn't object, how could she, even though she didn't believe his story and disliked the cat as soon as she grasped that the cat was really a proxy. Jerry had named the cat Nancy, and when Lily asked why Nancy, he shrugged and said, Why not, it's a name.

At her side, Jerry switched off the light and turned over, offering her his flannel pajama back and hugging sweetheart Nancy to his chest. Lily lay in the dark and turned her head toward the window. She couldn't actually see the window, the curtains were drawn because drawn curtains made Jerry feel closed-in and secure, but she looked at the window anyway and imagined what was beyond it, her vegetable garden and, farther out, the small, artificial pond and the goldfish in it. It was all ice now, it was winter, and sometimes, in the afternoon, she sat there, all bundled up, trying to glimpse a fish under the sheet of ice, wondering how they didn't freeze to death, for, come spring, there they were again, darting back and forth with their usual alert restiveness.

Another comfort were books, whatever Bertha, the librarian, recommended. When she wasn't cleaning or cooking or shopping or sitting by the pond, she sat on the screened-in porch, her feet up on the table, and read. She gave herself wholly to what she was reading, sometimes shedding real tears that came from deep inside, sometimes laughing out loud; she welcomed both the tears and the laughter.

As she was about to re-tally her day, other thoughts came, and she found herself engaged in the more difficult task of tallying up her life. They had been married seventeen years, no children—Jerry's sperm count was low, and so, alas, was his libido. A while back she had brought up the possibility of adoption, but Jerry said no, he had no desire raising someone else's unwanted drugged slip-up. Those were his words. Now she was pondering the question why she had given in to him so easily. The least she could have done was to put up a fight. She wasn't the fighting type, but still. It wasn't too late, though, she was only forty-two. She could either bring it up again, or simply leave him. An astonishing thought, but valid all the same. She could go back to work, the real-estate market was on fire, she would only need to renew her license, maybe take a short, refresher course.

Her friends, of course, would be shocked. "How come you never said anything?" they would say, accusingly. "We thought you and Jerry were love-birds. But, of course, we always knew you were hiding something. You're so secretive."

Secretive. That had been the consensus among her friends, but she wasn't really. Whenever she met a friend for lunch, or called her on the telephone, and before she had a chance to open her mouth and voice a complaint, or talk about something that troubled her, the friend, invariably, would preempt her with stories and complaints of her own, and by the time the friend was done recounting her woes, and Lily was done dispensing sympathy and sometimes advice, Lily was too exhausted to talk about herself, and that was why, essentially, she never got to reveal her secrets and so had earned the label "secretive," which, she had to admit, she kind of liked, it had a mystery to it, a kind of allure, a kind of suggestion that there was more to her than met the eye, and maybe there was.

Unless, of course, you stopped to think—as she sometimes did—why she didn't try harder, why she didn't assert herself and put her story forth, her friends would surely listen. Perhaps, she concluded, there was some truth to the label, maybe she was secretive, or maybe just passive, or maybe a combination of both. Her mother, in fact, had been secretive and cautious, telling Lily that the less people knew about you, the better.

You never knew when a friend would turn on you and reveal all that you had told her in confidence. Women, her mother had said, were a mean and deceiving lot. You were better off keeping away from their honey and their sting. "But we are women, too," Lily once countered, and her mother said, "Well, yes, we are."

And so, there were no easy answers. Her parents were dead, her husband slept witha cat, and she lay on her back, looking at a window behind a curtain and thinking thoughts that came to her randomly. She didn't pick them, she didn't invite them, they just came. It would have been better if they hadn't, if she could fall asleep just as easily as her husband.

She waited for him to start snoring, and presently he did. It was a light snore, it had a rhythm to it, grating and unpleasant to her ears, and it occurred to her that Nancy was also awake, listening, and that maybe Nancy, unlike Lily, found the snoring comforting.

Lily laughed softly. She could get herself a teddy bear and hug it while she slept. Jerry and his Nancy, she and her Teddy. A happy family sleeping together. Earlier, on the news, they talked about a man in Wyoming who went berserk and killed his wife then chopped her up and burned her parts in the fireplace, and Lily wondered what the body parts smelled like, and what kind of thoughts ran through the husband's head while the wife burned inthe fireplace. Possibly a fireplace the wife herself had paid for, or had helped pay for.

She also wondered if the husband sat in his armchair, or walked around the house while the wife burned. Maybe he spoke on the telephone with a friend, or a business associate.

He hadn't planned on getting caught, but he was. For the first time in his life, he scrapedand cleaned the fireplace, and dumped the ashes in a pond outside their home, but the police got him anyway.

There were many stories like that, men killing their wives, but fewer stories about women killing their husbands. Women who killed usually killed their children. The old story of good old Medea gone mad, temporarily. It was all temporary. Life was temporary, so you went a little nuts, so what? As long as you were able to come back to your senses, or your senses came back to you. If she had a child she would never dream of killing it, but she could dream of killing her husband. He wasn't a bad man, but he did have a cruel streak, which allowed him to boss her around and talk sharply to her when they had guestsat the table, as he did just this past Sunday. It was his fault that her love for him died, that her love had turned to hate. It was the kind of hate that made her blush when she becameaware of it, and she hated him all the more for having deposited such venom in her soul.

You have to allow people room to be mad in—Lily smiled in the dark. Things began to fall into place, they began to make sense. Yes, a room you could visit, and thenleave. A room to find strength in, then leave, strengthened. She must have visited such a room a few times in the past, and then reemerged, placid as ever. But now it was time to set her aims higher. Placid didn't satisfy her anymore. In fact, it bored her. She could easily get rid of Jerry, or, some accident might befall him as it did those who were complacent and indifferent to those around them. She would set Nancy loose on the quiet, placid neighborhood, sell the house and move on. Or, she might stay right where she was, keep Nancy and learn to love her as she once loved Jerry.

Yes, she saw it clearly. She was in the room now, asserting her will, inviting calamity on the one who deserved it. The one who deserved it was asleep, he would feel no pain, there would be no blood and no burning in the fireplace, but just a brief obituary in the *Daily Telegraph*, a black rectangle among all the other black rectangles, detailing the usual achievements and selfless contributions to the community. In the neat phrasing,the grief-stricken widow would get an honorable mention, as the one left behind, the one who survived the deceased, now living with a cat named Nancy.

The next day, at noon, she drove into town to meet Kate for lunch. Kate was late, as usual, but Lily didn't mind, it gave her time to study the menu, and the Specials board, and after a short debate, decide on the veal and string beans and mashed potatoes. "And extra gravy on the side," she rehearsed the line and tone of voice she would employ with the waiter when it was time to order.

Now that she was ready, she looked up and around her. The place was beginning to fill up, it was 12:45, and Kate was 15 minutes late. In a couple of minutes, Lily knew, Kate would come running into the restaurant, breathless, with an excuse and a story, but never an apology. And once she was done with that story, she would launch into another, and then another, and Lily would nod and smile, or wrinkle her brows in a show of sympathy and concern. But this time, Lily had resolved, she would tell Kate everything. She would tell her about the room, about her murderous thoughts, about wanting to leave Jerry. Kate was smart, she ran her own business from home, providing cleaning services to local offices and hotels. Tim, Kate's husband, was a respected lawyer, and they had two adorable girls, aged ten and twelve.

At the next table, five men in suits were ordering their lunch. Polite as anything, they held the open menus in their paws, looking up at the waiter, waiting their turn, and

Kate wondered if they were as polite and docile with their secretaries. She watched them, noting their thick necks, their pudgy, ringed digits, and loathed them for no reason at all, except that they wore suits, just like Jerry, and were heavyset and smug, also like Jerry.

She wasn't being fair, she knew that, but couldn't help herself. The only way she could forgive them would be to see them as pathetic, and feel sorry for them. And yet, like her, they were playing a role. What other choice did they have?

She looked at her watch: nearly one o'clock. Now the restaurant was packed, every seat was taken, except for Kate's. The waiter had come over a couple of times and she ordered a glass of white wine just to keep him happy, and still, no Kate. She took out her cell phone and, having ascertained she had no messages, called Kate and left a worried, hesitant message on her voicemail. When the waiter came over again, she apologized, paid her bill and went outside. She called Tim's office, but his secretary said he was in a meeting outside the office, and that she had no way of reaching him.

"But it's an emergency," Lily, helpless and close to tears, pleaded.

"I'm sorry," said the secretary. "What kind of an emergency?"

"It's about . . ." Lily hesitated. Maybe she was being hysterical. Kate was late, or maybe she forgot altogether that they had a lunch date.

"Never mind," she said and hung up. She waited till 1:15, anxiously scanning the street, the parking lot. No Kate. She got into her car and sat a moment, trying to decide if she should go home, or drive out to Kate's. It was a 30-minute drive, but, if she was truly worried about her friend, she should go out there to make sure that Kate was fine.

She should have ordered desert rather than wine, she thought as she drove to Kate's.

As the saying went, life was uncertain, eat the pudding first, and now, because of the wine, she felt a bit dizzy. Thank God she had some of the bread and butter the busboy had placed on the table. It was good bread, too, thick and crusty—She was tired. What was she doing, driving out to Kate's? And what if Kate wasn't home? What a waste this day was turning out to be. She would be better off going home and taking a short nap, even though, as a rule, she hardly ever took a nap. Such mid-day visits to the unconscious only made her feel even more tired. Tired and guilty, too, for having wasted valuable daylight time, but today, she thought, if she turned around and drove home, she would take a nap, if just this once.

Lily pulled to the side of the road and again tried Kate's home number, as well asher cell phone, and got Kate's cheerful message. She drove on. She was almost there, she might as well continue.

Finally, as she pulled into the driveway, she noticed Kate's car, and breathed a sigh of relief. At least, she'd get to see her friend, sit for a while in her kitchen and devour a quick, improvised lunch before heading home. Her spirits revived to the point of near-joy, Lily got out of the car and hurried up the path, but, as she approached the door, she began to wonder why Kate, who was obviously home, hadn't answered the phone. She rang the bell and waited, then rang again.

Fear and anxiety pulled in her stomach. She tried the door, but it was locked. She went around the house and tried the back door, but it, too, was locked. She cupped her hands and looked through the glass, but couldn't see very far beyond the kitchen. All she saw was the long, granite counter, the fridge, and a strip of the black and white tiled floor.

The interior seemed desolate, dim and abandoned, as if no one lived there.

You're being absurd, she muttered to herself as she dialed 911, then sat down on the front steps, waiting for the police. She found a hard candy in her purse and sucked on it, hoping it would expunge the odor of wine from her breath. A bright cold sun stood high in the sky, blinding her. She wanted to curl up and sleep, right there, on the stoop, but soon, a cruiser pulled to the curb, and two tall officers got out and walked toward her. She rose to her feet and haltingly introduced herself, and then told them about the lunch, about how unlike it was for Kate to be late, and not to answer the phone. Kate lived by the phone, it was part of her job. And so, she must be inside, they must break the door.

"We can't just break into people's homes," one of the officers said. Both of them seemed young, in their twenties, but the one who spoke seemed a bit older.

"I understand that," she said, patiently at first, then let her voice rise in tandem with her mounting fear and frustration. "This is an emergency. Better safe than sorry, don't you agree? I'll pay for the damage, all it would take is for you to break the glass. I could have done it myself, but I called you. We're losing precious time. Her husband is unreachable, she is unreachable, which is highly unusual. I'm not some crazy woman off the street, I'm a friend of the family. I know that something dreadful has happened, I just know it!" she screamed. "I just know it!"

Something in her voice must have alarmed them. One of them went back to the car and spoke on the radio, while she paced back and forth, wringing her hands, waiting for the officer who stayed with her to try and calm her, but, she realized, he was the younger one, perhaps new on the job, and seemed more bewildered than concerned.

After what seemed like an awful long time, the other officer returned, handing her a clipboard. "Please sign this," he said.

"What's that?"

"Permission for us to break in."

She signed the form with a trembling hand and hurried toward the back, with the two officers following behind. Now they seemed as worried as she was, and it pleased her. With no effort at all, they picked the lock, and the door opened, smoothly, soundlessly.

"Kate?" Lily called, walking through the kitchen and into the open living room.

"Kate? Maybe upstairs," she said, glancing back at the officers and turning toward the staircase.

"Wait." The older officer stopped her. "Let us go first. You wait here."

She continued to pace, then poured herself a glass of water and sat down on the couch, feeling faint. What was taking them so long? She leaned back and shut her eyes, then opened them again. Her head was buzzing with radio static and voices, then sirens out on the street, and the young officer running down the stairs and opening the front door.

She wanted to get up, but couldn't, her blood had frozen solid, and she was shaking all over, as if with high fever. She was hallucinating. Men in white burst into the living room and up the stairs, and people were shouting and pointing, and she just sat there, invisible and unnoticed.

Where are the girls? She wondered, then remembered Kate saying something abouta school field trip. She draped her arms around her knees, let her head drop, and was soon sobbing, hard sobs that wrenched her guts and sent spasms down her back. What if she had gone home instead of driving here and getting the police? Someone sat down on the couch and put a comforting arm around her, talking to her in hushed tones, telling her everything was going to be all right, her friend was going to make it, no need to cry.

She looked up. It was another officer, older, kinder, maybe the captain, maybe the one in charge. He was still talking, and she watched his lips move. "You did well," he said.

"You saved a life." She thought she saw tears in his eyes.

"I'm so tired," she said. "And so hungry. I didn't have lunch."

The officer laughed. "You'll come with us to the station, and we'll get you the best lunch this town has to offer."

Yes, she thought, the best lunch this town has to offer. "How's Kate?"

"She'll be fine." He patted her hand. "She lost a lot of blood, but she was conscious and alert enough to tell us who did this to her."

"Did what to her?"

The officer looked at her. "He hit her over the head with a brick, and left her to bleed to death. Broke a window upstairs and made a bit of a mess to make it look like a burglar had done it. Very banal, but he couldn't have known that you would enter the picture. Yet another perfect murder gone imperfect. And, most importantly, thanks to you the woman is still alive. Usually, we arrive too late."

"But why?" Lily asked, shaking her head and speaking like an automaton. "We all thought they had a perfect partnership, a perfect marriage."

"Well," the officer said.

That night, Lily and Jerry ate out. I can't kill him, Lily thought while chewing her delicious fillet mignon. I can't kill him, but I can certainly leave him. Which she did. Next morning, she filed for a divorce and a restraining order, and, with her name all over the news as the brave, resourceful woman who had saved a friend's life, and with Chief O'Brien on her side, it was Jerry, not Lily, who had to leave the house and move into a motel, instructed not to come within 500 yards of his estranged wife. Nancy also remained in the house, and when Kate was released from the hospital, the three of them celebrated together with champagne and caviar and Cat Chow.

MODERN ART OR
LIVING WITH A NUMBER

Every time she bought a new painting she was a little tipsy. It gave her a good feeling, going up to the painter at a gallery opening, pointing at a painting and saying, I fancy this one. It made her feel important, but, she assured herself, not in the haughty, often nasty manner the real important people had of making others feel small.

She said that line twice in the past six months, the first one when she bought a quite large painting of wild and exotic and mildly threatening flowers, and the second, when she bought a medium size painting depicting old-fashioned, canvas lounge chairs on a beach on the Italian Riviera. The chairs had purple and yellow stripes and, unlike the threatening flowers, seemed cheerful, even frivolous, and that's why she went up to the artist and pointed and said her line.

These two new purchases now hung on her walls, the flowers in her bedroom, the chairs in her living room, and every night, before falling asleep, she looked at the flowers, and every morning, while sitting at her desk, she looked at the chairs. It also happened that the flowers appeared in her dreams, but never, as yet, the chairs on the beach.

On both gallery visits, she had a glass of wine in her hand, the second or third, and, on her brain, the image of a lit cigarette she could not actually have, since the prohibition laws had gone into effect.

And, it so happens that her first novel had just been published, and she had come into some money thanks to her uncle, the last surviving member of her family, who had died in the spring, and so, in some respects, she was on a roll.

"When it rains, it pours," she would say to friends, shrugging, as one trying to make light of it all. At home, hiding, she thought of herself as one living with a number, the Amazon.com ranking number, which told her if her book was in the dumps, or, on a good day, sold a few copies. Every night before falling asleep she decided she must never look at it again, at the number, and must also discard the digital scale on her bathroom floor, but every morning, a tabula rasa, a kind of virgin all over again, she did, faithfully, check on her weight and on her book.

She was weak, and she accepted it as an irredeemable fact at the very moment she stood on the scale, or when typing Amazon's URL. When night came, she was strong again, determined, even vowing to stop smoking. She also vowed she would be more generous, more accepting. She would stop rushing and worrying, she would have sex with the first man who offered, she would start a new novel. Yes, she would.

Living with a number reminded her of one of her most cherished novels, Jiri Weil's *Living with a Star*. And, of course, it reminded her of her uncle, the one who had died. He, too, had lived with a number, a blue one, tattooed on his arm. A free tattoo, he liked to shout, and German-made, no less! She loved her uncle, her mother's brother, he was irreverent, he was different, he never married. In many ways he was like her, or she was like him, or, more like him than like her parents who had cherished peace and quiet and security more than anything, if only for her sake.

It was night again, she was going through her resolutions, but not with the usual ardor. Earlier, she had gone to yet another opening, bought yet another painting, a small self-portrait of the newly deceased artist. Before she bought it, she stood and looked into the small eyes of the artist, now three weeks dead. She looked at him, and he looked straight back at her.

Whose life am I living? She asked him, mutely. Around her, the usual set of the up and coming talked with much exuberance; the dead artist was forgotten, even as his portrait hung on the wall, and she felt bad for him, missing his own opening. He seemed vigorous, in his 50's or 60's, it was hard to tell for sure, and she tried to imagine what he felt when he put life into the small dark eyes that stared right back at him as he painted them. It would give her, she thought, a kind of vertigo, but then, she was not a painter.

She went up to the gallery owner, a brisk brunette in her 40's or 50's, it was hard to tell for sure, quite tall on her sharp stiletto heels, which could be used, in case of an emergency, as a stabbing tool, and said, "I want that one," pointing at the small self-portrait. Later, feeling a little tipsy and therefore rebellious, she went into a stall in the ladies room, placed the glass of wine on the floor and lit a cigarette.

Long inhale. That wonderful buzz in the head. The artist, she ruminated further, reminded her of her uncle, and so, the three of them would live together, quietly, away from the noise, away from the crowds. No more gallery openings, she resolved. No more paintings, no more pretense, no more—

"Someone's smoking in here, who's smoking?" The harsh voice of the gallery owner broke into her pleasant reveries.

"It's me, Vera," Vera said in a small voice.

"I don't care who you are." A pause. "Which Vera? Do I know you?" A softening of tone.

"Yes, Vera, I just bought a painting, the self-portrait?" Coyly, a deliberate stab at false humility.

"Oh, yes. Well, you know, smoking is forbidden. Fire regulations, and so on. We have to be careful."

"I know, I'm truly sorry, I'm quitting anyway." She bent over and picked up the wine glass from the floor. She was a bit disoriented still, perhaps shamed, and the glass, somehow, slipped from her fingers, forming a collection of reddish glistening shards on the black-and-white tile floor, a new kind of artwork, a kind of kaleidoscope only she could admire.

"Are you all right in there?" A shuffle of the stiletto heels.

"Yes, yes, I'll be right out."

She waited a few moments, then came out of the stall, taking small, hesitant steps. Thankfully, the gallery owner was gone. She picked up the shards with paper towels and, when she was done cleaning, she sneaked out through the back door as befits a criminal on the run.

It was still early, only eight o'clock, and a chattering human river streamed on either side of her. She maintained her balance and a steady step. She was a mess, but only in her head, and, of course, she had an excuse. Her Amazon number had been climbing lately and she couldn't think of ways to bring it down, of ways to keep her book alive in people's minds.

Ah, well, she thought, a number was only a number. Her novel was only a novel, one of many. All these people, rushing past her, didn't live with a number. They lived joyously, or so it seemed on this beautiful fall night. Change was in the air, even she could smell it. The artist was dead, her uncle was dead, but she was alive. Soon, the self-portrait would hang on her wall, and she would start a new life. She would stop checking on the number, she would not get on the scale, and maybe, just maybe, she would quit smoking once and for all.

MEN AT WORK

It is Saturday morning in New York City. A woman sits at her desk, facing the large windows that make her part of the world. She wants to read, but N sneaks uninvited into her thoughts, just as M does. This is quite disturbing, for M and N are two different men, one of whom is her husband, now on leave of absence from their marriage.

She sat herself at her desk, determined to read and not worry about a thing. After all, it was morning again. When her husband was around, she would jump out of bed on Saturday mornings and rummage through the apartment in a frenzied, calculated plan to do away with the dust. Her husband would move listlessly in bed, watching her clean around him. Why, he would wonder aloud, must she do it now, so early in the morning? If she lingered in bed for a while, he would help her take care of the dust. Why couldn't she wait?

She wondered about this herself, but to him she would say that she wanted these chores behind her, and so have the rest of the day to herself.

That industrious woman was me. The funny thing is that after he left, I became my old self again, blind to dust and stains. Now that he is gone, I linger in bed for a while, then slowly make my way to the bathroom where, first thing, I bring my face close to the mirror, looking for a change for the better that might have occurred in my sleep. What I see will determine my mood for the day. I then let the water run in the shower and wake up to it. This morning I cleaned myself inside and out, but I can still smell N on my skin, N who had spent the night and fled in the morning, fearing that if he stayed a minute longer I might propose to him.

M and N, N and M. Who are they? Who comes first?

Why are my windows bare and dirty? I can answer that. They are bare because I don't want curtains to obstruct the view. And dirty? Well, dirty because they haven't been cleaned since M cleaned them two years ago with the enthused excitement of moving into a new place. He also hung white, lacy curtains, now stored away in a closet.

Through the dusty glass the world outside is an old photograph, crumpling at the edges. At night, though, it's much better. The dust disappears, and the scenery takes on a more promising, enchanting look. Lights in the distance twinkle and hint at secret activities. A moving figure behind a dimly lit window across the street opens up a whole world of speculations.

Right now, the white chunks of smoke that regretfully leave their chimneys and drift eastward, are the only indication that life is on, that the system is still working, which is a good sign. My prime occupation these days is looking for and collecting good signs.

Another good sign are the ropes hanging outside my windows. They have been there all week and my practical mind tells me that they are there for a reason, that work is being done on the facade of the building. Somebody cares. M wouldn't know it, he hasn't been here for a while. He may come back and find a completely different building, recognizable only by its number. He may come back and find a completely different tenant living in this apartment. Anything can happen in the city. This is something everyone knows, even M, who seems so remote. When we first met, I was convinced his eyes were made of glass, blue and icy. Later, I became convinced that I could make those eyes change color, so when he suggested marriage, I said, All right, let's do it.

It was quite simple, really, and a good idea at the time. Then M came up with another idea: Live apart from one another for a while. At first

I thought it was a good idea. Since then, I've had to remind myself that living alone has its advantages. Being a romantic, I can perfect my sense of uniqueness and live in glorious solitude. I don't have to worry about anyone's but my own laundry. I can prepare the salad dressing to suit my taste buds. I can read in bed late at night with no one there to complain about the light. And if M never comes back, then M never comes back. And if I fall in love with N, or with someone else, then I fall in love with N, or with someone else. End of book one.

I grab a pen in a sudden determination to write a letter. I can write M and alert him to all these possibilities. But then, he knows them. I can write and demand a divorce. I can also write N and ask why he left in such a hurry.

M and N, N and M. Funny little men, each with his own set of problems. Funny funny funny. Both men spell confusion. Stability is out of the question; something always threatens to fall apart.

It is a bright Saturday morning. If the phone rings, I will answer it immediately. If I wean myself of M and N, I will enjoy reading my book. If I were a more mature person, I would be better at handling the situation. Instead, I just sit and stare at the ropes, which magically begin to rattle. Something is happening out there. Voices are coming from somewhere and nowhere.

I perk in my seat. Do I hear Spanish? The ropes squeak and, for a brief, absurd moment I feel I'm a goddess, watching two figures emerge and appear before me: first the heads, then the shoulders, torsos and thighs, and finally the feet, steadfast on a large wooden board. Two strong male bodies. They have worked themselves up to my windows, these messengers of good will. I bestow a divine smile on them, but they don't see me, yet. Were they to arrive a bit later, they would have found a topless deity seated at her desk, her shirt tossed off to welcome the sun now reaching her windows full blast.

Yes, it's definitely Spanish. They shout to each other against the wind and look down to the street below. Together we form a perfect triangle of which I am the culminating point. They steady themselves on the board and turn, a smile on their faces. Two happy jolly men, caught in my magnetic field. They freeze, their eyes interlocked with mine.

They say hello.

I nod. I don't want to appear too eager.

They exchange a quick glance and say something in Spanish, their voices and manner subdued. Are they embarrassed by my presence? Do they expect me to disappear so they can work in peace? I hope not. I want them to feel comfortable. I put a smile on my face, but they're already bent over their buckets, dipping their brushes in paint. They have probably noticed the dust on the windows, on the shelves, and concluded there's nothing here for them but sorrow and disrepair. They will do their work hurriedly and zoom up to the next floor.

I watch them and review the moment. I sit, they stand. I hold a pen, they hold a brush. I twiddle my time away, they work. Their brushes move with ease, the paint is black, thick and obedient. My pen is still, its ink black, but not obedient. The two men are muscular and virile, but also soft. They risk their lives for me, their faces stern, their movements quick and confident. Two high priests at work.

I like the smell of paint. I smile at them.

One of them smiles back. He is slim and is taller than the other man. His brush tickles the brick, and he begins to whistle to its rhythm. He knows what he is doing, he knows his work. He has a good body, a firm body, the body of a builder, a fighter, the body of a man. The other one is chubby in a sweet sort of way. Are they married? Probably, with a few kids running about, livening up the household. The wife cleans the windows and cooks the meals. After a hard day's work, the husband returns home. He is tired, but content. The kids run to him. He lifts the smallest one up high in the air. The little one shrieks with delight. The mother appears at the door, wiping her hands on the white apron. They kiss and enter the house. He takes a shower, she hands him a clean shirt. They kiss again and sit down to eat. They are five at the table and conversation is flowing. Laughter rings in the air. The food is simply prepared and is tasty. The kids are put to bed. Husband and wife retire to the master bedroom. Their love-making is good and wholesome. They fall asleep. Another day is over.

I sigh.

The whistler is waving a dollar bill at me. How long has he been waving like this? I look at him through dreamy eyes, my lips pursed in a gentle, questioning smile. Do I appear baffled enough, innocent enough? Can he tell I'm soft, tender, loving and alone? He says he wants to come in through the window, is it all right with me? He says he wants to go downstairs and get some coffee for himself and his friend. He has a heavy Spanish accent, and his voice is strong and melodious. In his eagerness to make himself understood, he puts one foot on the ledge of the window and shows me the dollar bill. I resist a compelling urge to lower my gaze to his culminating point. Is he aware of it? I must keep my associations clean, otherwise I will blush, which is a womanly thing to do, but only at the right time.

The whistler, though, is an innocent, not a seducer. Without words he tells me that his intentions are clean and straightforward. All he wants is to go downstairs and buy coffee.

I understand. I get up and push the window open. I hesitate for only a moment, then offer to make coffee for him and his friend. It's a practical suggestion. It will save him a trip down a slow elevator, and, it will also save him a dollar. The whistler says something to the other one in Spanish. The man looks at me shyly and smiles. He is a kind and sensitive man, easygoing and affectionate. He can play for hours with his daughter, and there's nothing he wouldn't do for his wife. His dark brown eyes tell me that.

The whistler turns to me with a smile, and the dollar bill disappears in his pocket. In unison they tell me that I'm sweet. I smile in response and go to the kitchen. I put water on the stove and fiddle with the sugar bowl. What else do I need? Milk. I open the refrigerator; it's so embarrassingly desolate inside. It used to be packed when we were two in the kitchen. M loves to experiment with food. N, too, is a very good cook. He left his wife and children, and now cooks gourmet for his friends on the weekends. He even grows basil in his garden.

I take out the milk container and place it on the counter next to the coffee jar and the sugar bowl. Everything is ready except for the water. I can hide in the kitchen and wait for it to boil, or, I can go back to my desk and sit down. It's my apartment, and I don't know these men. If they crossed my way on the street, I probably wouldn't see them. The streets are filled with strangers. And lawyers. N is one of them, and when I call him I get his secretary. The attorney is busy, he will call you back, she says. Thank you, I say. You're welcome, she says, and we hang up.

I go to my desk and sit down. In my short absence, the two men have arranged themselves comfortably and settled down on either side of the board that wheels them up and down. Apparently, they have decided to take a break on my floor. They sit with their backs to me, facing the great vastness of rooftops, the sun, and wait for my coffee. The whistler lights a cigarette and, as an afterthought, turns around, seeking me. He blinks, surprised to find me so close to them, right behind them, just sitting there so quietly. He hastens to offer me a Camel, and I get up and go to the window, even though I'm trying to quit, and Camels are much too strong. M smokes menthols, which are also too strong, and N doesn't smoke at all, except for an occasional joint. He is cool.

The whistler lights a match, and I bend out the window toward him. The wind blows it, and he smiles. I blush. He strikes another match, and I bend again. Our heads touch, and for a moment we form a small, protected sphericity. Mission completed, the whistler turns to his friend, and I turn to my CD player. Waiting to be played is a CD M gave me as a present for our third, perhaps last, wedding anniversary. It's Maria Callas singing *La Traviata*. I melt every time I listen to it, but my friends the painters don't even acknowledge the music. I march off to the kitchen and watch the cigarette burn in the ashtray, remembering how I blushed when the whistler put a match to my cigarette. A smile sneaks to my lips. I can invite the whistler and his friend to my bedroom. They're on a break anyway. The whole affair shouldn't take too long, and we could cherish our daring for the rest of our lives. They could tell their friends about it over a mug of beer on a Sunday afternoon, while their wives fussed over barbecued spareribs. I could discuss it with M and N. This will give a hell of a shock to M, and will surprise N. They will finally realize that they are dealing with an unpredictable, all-powerful woman, a woman of mystery and multiple existence, the Femme Fatale of all time, the all-consuming Black Widow. They will lose their heads and fight over me. I'll become notorious. I'll have to consult my calendar before committing myself. Life will be what it was meant to be.

I sigh and open the cupboard. I choose two cups and make sure they are clean. I have two guests on my windowsill, and I don't want to offend them with neglect. My guests want milk and sugar in their coffees. They didn't specify quantities to me, and so, as a good and loving wife, I approximate their tastes to mine and decide how much milk, how many spoons of sugar will satisfy them. When they sit there, sipping my coffee, it will dawn on them that I care.

What am I going to do with them once we are in the bedroom?

Naturally, they will have to take the initiative. They are the men, I am the woman. They will have to be imaginative, inventive. They will gather up momentum and inspiration as we proceed, drawing confidence from one another. After all, they are two, and I am one. I'll do my share. I'll moan, I'll bend this way and that. We'll move with ease in perfect rhythm, their pulse harmonious with mine. Time for sure will be arrested, but we'll have to part sooner or later, they'll have to go home to the dinner table. I'll see them to the windows and gracefully wave, as they wheel themselves down and away.

The water boils, and I come out of the kitchen, two cups of coffee in my hands. I approach the windows very slowly, a broad smile on my face, careful not to spill a drop; this should indicate to them that I'm a conscientious housekeeper after all. My jaw begins to hurt, but I keep on smiling. Observing myself through a third eye, I see a sorceress who has flavored the hot, steaming coffee with a potent potion, then lured these two innocents into her cave.

I'm bad, bad, bad.

The whistler gets up, and the board moves with him. He holds on to the rope, and I extend the coffee cups out the open window. He gets hold of one cup, then the other. He smiles, the chubby one smiles. I smile and go to the kitchen to get my own cup. The three of us sit and sip our coffees. They no longer sit with their backs to me, and now I have their profiles. They're both dark-haired, they both wear a mustache. Do I like mustaches? Sometimes. On them they look good. They ask for my name, and I tell them. They are Joe and Mike. Joe and Mike are different from M and N. M is blondish, N is silvery.

M and N do not have mustaches; they shave every morning.

Joe does most of the talking. He is the slim, slender whistler. He should be in the movies. He is animated, he talks with his hands, his eyes glow with conviction. I don't understand a word he says. He is talking to Mike who, intermittently, smiles and nods. The sun is directly on us, and I feel hot and sticky. Of course, I could take off my shirt, as I normally do, but the sight might stun my painters, and they'll stagger off the board to their certain death. My head swims with the flow, and M and N are pushed to a dark corner, having diminished in size and bulk. They are two eerie midgets, straining to regain their former stature.

Joe turns to me, and I ask him what exactly are they doing. His answer comes swiftly. They are painting the frames of the windows this time around. Later in the week they will paint the whole side of the building to make it look nice for nice girls like me. I nod, and Joe asks what I do. He says it looks like I'm a designer or something, and he points at the drawing table near the desk. Oh, I say, this is my husband's.

Oh, you're married, Joe says. That's good, that's very good. Marriage is a good thing, Joe says, and I smile brightly at him.

Joe and Mike get up. They pass their empty cups through the window and thank me again. I wave feebly as they wheel themselves out of sight, up to the next floor. See you later, Joe shouts, and they are gone. Dangling ropes are the only remnants of my two Spanish men, now on their way to the nurse who lives upstairs with her two dogs.

Silence descends. My gaze shifts, and I watch myself in a photograph laid underneath the plastic cover on the desk. M put it there. Ms and Ns, their doubts and aches, were unknown to me then, unsuspected. I was a virgin, just starting out, my first boyfriend standing next to me, protective, looking straight ahead. I look away, my lips slightly parted. Was I saying something, or was I posing for the camera?

AS OF A NIGHT

A woman without a man is like a fish without a bicycle—
Gloria Steinem

Every so often she got stoned to loud music, sometimes country, some-times rock. Every so often she got off the couch and swayed melanchol-ically to the music, letting her head roll from side to side. Melancholy, she thought, becomes me. Too bad no one is here to see it, to see me in it. And yes, she liked the way her thoughts looped and swirled according to their own whimsy or program. And yes, too bad no one was there to see it. Our best moments gone unseen. C'est la vie, oui, oui.

Yes, she knew French, she was a francophone, a faux-French. A disgrace these days with a Bushie and a Dickie in Washington, D.C. Derelict City. Yes, dereliction is a way of life in our capital city, and her life as well was an open-ended dereliction. A life of scheduling, routinely, then loosening the noose a bit.

Open, and ended. And a bit of a twirl—voilà, another French word. How fast and deep are you willing to reveal your wonderful self? When your door is locked? Do you even know who your next-door neighbor is? Perhaps the one who would finally proffer his other cheek?

Maybe you are hungry? Yes, you are! But, stop the party? Because your tummy cries food?

And her dancing shadow on the wall. And the song, and the music, and the cry, and the vague longing, and the need, made of the moment.

It is all of the moment. You take it in, and then you let go, retaining something, possibly the essence. And up in the sky a full but a watery moon and, like last night, aloof.

Very profound, this. She was getting more profound by the pound, no, by the minute. C'est la vie. Sa vie. She was on the verge of forgiving herself, tout. At least for the moment. At least for the now. She was not one to worry about the order of things and other such perishables. When she worried, she worried about the small things. A friend of hers said it was because of the Holocaust, because her parents were survivors, Holocaust survivors. That particular friend blamed it all on the Holocaust, but she, the one who could, said, No, it's not the Holocaust.

She ate her meals on the floor, on the carpet, because it felt ceremoniously foolish to sit alone at the ornate dinner table. And, no matter what others might say about the matter, she was convinced she enjoyed her food as much as anyone. Even if she ate on the floor, hunched over her plate of salad and spaghetti, and then straightening up for the chewing and swallowing.

Besides, she liked to watch something while she ate and, eating at the table, she'd see only the faint reflection of her image in the thick glass of the tabletop. Having her dinner on the carpet she watched TV, like many others in fact, and followed the story of the hour with the insatiable appetite of a scandalmonger.

The fact was, she had met a man the night before, and was now thinking about him, even though she didn't want to think about him. The Split / Conflicted Brain Syndrome. She worked the acronym in her head, hoping for some musicality that would prove it had been in the cards that the two of them should meet.

She didn't want to think about him because she wasn't sure whether she really liked him, or just wanted to be coupled. All night last night, on her couch, she said that, and he said that, and she said that, and then he, in response to a question, said something quite profound, which she tried to remember now and couldn't, but she did remember appreciating his answer, for it was an answer concerning her—of this she was certain. She thought it profound because it surprised her, it went in a direction she hadn't anticipated. A question she had asked in all innocence, and he had answered in all seriousness, the seriousness of a first date, of getting to know you, of wanting to like you, of wanting to impress you, of wanting to spend time with you, in bed, and outside it.

Inside and out. Simple, and yet intricate and potentially disturbing. Maybe profound! She had the sense that he was a nester, a man who needed a lot and therefore got himself a dog and a cat. She had the sense that he had suffered at the hands and mouths of women, and that he sought such women out.

He was good-looking, she had to admit that her heart and eyes and mind, in some order or other, responded as soon as she saw him in the room. It was Christmas dinner with old friends, and she didn't expect any surprises, no newcomer. But there he was, like a lost cowboy, a last-minute addition, so said the hostess in a whisper, a long-gone cousin who had suddenly reappeared and had to be invited. After all, they were family, however distant.

The "distant" part got her approving attention instantly. No exchange of gossip between prospective lover and inquisitive cousin-hostess, who would be eager to know all the dirty details about and from both sides. With all good intentions, of course, with all good and best wishes.

I bruise easily, she told him at some point, meaning that her skin was delicate and bruisable, but, as she heard herself speak the words, she realized he might interpret her meaning differently, and yet she couldn't think of a way to amend the words that had already come out of her mouth. Still, she felt certain that whatever meaning he gleaned from her words, her manner told him that she was keeping all escape routes open.

At her door, as they were saying good night and goodbye—it was high time, 3am—and she extended her hand, and he took it, she wished him a happy new year and leaned forward, seeking his cheek, but he, mistaking her intention, and eager as well—it showed on his face—and surprised by this sudden gesture on her part, also leaned forward, offering his lips, then realizing, in a flash, it was the cheek she wanted, and he offered it, making a quick, perhaps disappointed, adjustment.

In bed, after he left, she read for a while, forgetting all about him, and then fell asleep and into a long, tortuous dream, where she and he are making love, or trying to, but, intermittently, he takes off and flies in the air, performing tricks for her, perhaps to amuse her, perhaps to annoy her, so she tries to fly, too, and, to her great astonishment, she succeeds, she flies in the air, and does all sorts of cat-woman acrobatics, but, as she flies, she tells herself, This is all unreal, as she knows herself incapable of flying.

She woke up from the dream disheveled and broken and fearful, blaming the drinks they had had at the dinner party, and the pot they had smoked when they sat on her couch.

She didn't like to fret, but fretting was part of her makeup. Fretting and debating and analyzing and second-guessing herself. And also listening to oldies on the radio late at night, like, for instance, to Sinatra singing, That Old Black Magic. American singers, she believed, poured their hearts out, more so than their European counterparts, who were, on the whole, more circumspect in their delivery. She wanted to believe that she was, in many respects, just like everyone else, corny and senti-mental and pining after something or someone, or the idea of someone in the abstract, a being she didn't bother to endow with the prerequisite look and intelligence, but someone who already came custom-made, so she could get right down to business and imagine the very first witty conversation they would have.

How frank and honest and candid can you be? The first time? How far would you go? Would you reveal your inner self? Like, your real real inner self?

She swayed to the music. Her life, if she had to sum it up, wasn't all that bad. Like everyone else, she had her moments. Her generous moments, her loving moments, her bad moments. She liked late-night radio because it was then when they played the best music, the best songs. Or, this was how she heard them, late at night, when the streets were quiet, and she was alone, finally alone.

SPIDERS

'Cut it, woman,' said her guest; and the 'woman' cut it accordingly.
Had she followed her inclinations, she would have cut the person also.
Shirley: a tale/ Charlotte Bronte

Arachnologists tell us that for most species in nature, a husband's place is in the digestive tract of his wife. I know very little about nature, let alone spiders, but I do know about husbands (three so far) and stomachs. As a little girl of five, I said to my mother: "If you put a dime in my palm every time you tell me that a way to a man's heart is through his stomach, when I'm eighteen I'll have a nice dowry to catch him with." My mother laughed and stroked my hair and said I'd grow up to be a bookkeeper. And she was right! I work for Lilinbaum & Lilinbaum and make a good enough living, and with money collected from my exes and wisely invested, I'm not poor.

As an aside, let me provide a short and relevant history: my first two exes perished under my care. The third, a mistake and a virtual cliché, eloped with a cleaning lady from Guatemala.

Still, I'm not content. At moments of respite, like now, I sit in the cafeteria of L&L and, over a modest lunch of greens, I ponder when and how we veered off nature's path. I watch my fellow-workers (yes, most of them are fellows) in their suits and brown shoes and eat my heart out. It's silly and futile, but I can't help it. In my own small way I'm a scientist, a kind of an investigator (instigator!). I watch them and conclude: They don't look it, but they must be clever. Or, more clever than us females. For, excluding my own quite satisfying record, if anyone ends up in the digestive tract of the other, it is usually the female in the male's. And then, just like that, it hit me: God exists! And, since He made man in His own image, He was naturally sympathetic to male issues, displaying a characteristic ambivalence toward females, whores and saints alike.

I sneaked a glance around me. Great revelations pulsed through me, and I wondered if their impact showed on my face. My boss was sitting at the next table, leafing through a brochure and cuddling his balls under the napkin. Ours was an open and tolerant firm, all creeds and religions were revered, and every Friday at 4pm, we gathered in the board room for a toast and a brief, open-ended prayer.

As an aside, let me admit right here lest I forget: If I had balls, I'd be cuddling them , too, for they are soft and bouncy and always handy.

It was only Monday, and here I was, awash in religious awakenings. I wanted to stand up and reveal myself, share what I had just experienced, but common sense—the proverbial: "There's a time for everything"— prevailed. I finished my salad, then joined my boss for an exploratory chat. He had just divorced his wife (no one knew why), and I thought I might as well get started on number four.

BULLY

Iraq Chaos Dims Bush's Vision of Democracy in Mideast —headline news

"Learn to be a bully," she reads in a magazine while waiting for her gynecologist. As usual, the doctor is running late. "An emergency," the receptionist says when she inquires how much longer she'll have to wait, an answer she'd expected, they always use the same line, the same lie. But, she says nothing. Like a sweet and docile lamb she goes back to her seat and continues to wait like the other women in the room who looked up when she went to the receptionist and listened to the exchange, hoping perhaps she'd go berserk on their behalf, scream her head off, yelling that she is sick and tired of waiting, her time is just as valuable as the doctor's! She is worn-out, listening to lies about emergencies, about insurgents and surges and timelines and terrorists and presidential hopefuls. She is tired of visions dimmed in chaos, and chaos dimmed in visions. Not to mention the billions spent, the thousands killed in the fakery of freedom. Not to mention American Idol and CSI. How much longer of this poppycock? How much longer, for God's sake?

But the receptionist is just as tired, she's seen it all, she's heard it all, she has her own problems, not to mention that on top of everything else, she has to cover for her boss the doctor, it's part of the job.

So, take a deep breath and keep quiet. We're all trapped. Take a deep breath and keep quiet. Pick up the magazine and learn how to be a bully.

Is a bully at hand better than two bullies in the bush? Are two bullies in Washington better than a bully in Iraq?

A dead bully? In the eyes of God, is a Christian bully better than a bully of lesser faiths? Is God a bully who loves bullies? Gynecologists?

Endless, she thinks, endless. She may sit in the room for another thirty or forty minutes, while the good doctor cashes in, but, at the very least, her mind is engaged in eternal questions.

At last, she is called into the inner sanctum, disrobes, the doctor pokes in her vagina, all is well, her womanly organs are well formed and well behaved, at least for the moment. "Go home, you're healthy, enjoy life," he tells her, offering a wry smile.

THE ART OF LIVING

She had gone to bed at 11 p.m. and woke up at 2 a.m., five hours too early. Unable to fall asleep again, she rose, rinsed the dinner dishes in the sink, and prepared breakfast: coffee and half a scone she found in the fridge. While eating, she read a novel about a young British couple, living in Rome. She didn't believe a word she read, the author—British, Male, White (BMW, she named him)—was too glib and "cute" in his assertions, but she had to press on and take notes for the review she had been commissioned to write. In the back of her mind, the thought lurked that she might call friends and alert them to the fact that she was awake. Instead, breakfast over, she put the novel aside and went to her desk.

Dear World, she wrote in her journal. You're so peaceful and still at this hour, so quiet. What if the End were to arrive, and I'd be the only one to witness it?

Observing the dark sky and the few distant stars, Cookie considered: A jetlag even though she didn't travel? Or, perhaps, she did travel. All day long, she cruised on her impressions, which took her places. The seemingly aimless, schedule-less days of a free-lancer, did qualify as space travel. She was a kind of space cadet—some people, those who had jobs, thought this of her, not realizing she saw it in their eyes; discreet, they sought to hide it from her.

At 3a.m. she was hungry again and went into the kitchen for inspiration. A toast. And avocado, she decided, already savoring the avocado on her tongue. As an afterthought, she added a slice of tomato on top of the toast and avocado and sprinkled some salt on it. All things considered, being hungry was a good sign. It meant she was hungry for the things of life. Her mother, she remembered, loved avocado. When her mother was alive, Cookie hated avocado, but now she loved it. We're all emotional orphans, she thought, chewing.

At 4 a.m., she went back to bed, still reading BMW. Soon she tired of him, turned off the light and lay in the dark, watching a vision of herself, spread-eagle on her wide white bed, floating over the city, over the skyscrapers, and calling out to her friends.

HELLO AND THANK YOU!

The night before Christmas Eve, feeling a bit aimless, she decided to go out for a walk, and then, without thinking, walked into a crowded bar, perhaps to escape the cold, perhaps hoping for the good, old generics of noise and company. Miraculously, a man was getting up from his stool, and she quickly claimed it, congratulating her propitious timing, and, in her heart, she also thanked the man who had warmed up the seat for her. He was a large man, and his rump had generously covered the entire leather square. She ordered a shot of her favorite French brandy—Raynal—a luxury she allowed herself only rarely, and sat there, sipping, thawing, trying to look chipper and jovial like the rest of them. She signaled the bartender and ordered another shot. What would happen if she were to light up? The question lit up in her brain, and a small, drunken smile appeared on her lips. Would they arrest her? Cigarettes in the city had been criminalized, which made her resent the city and those who ran it, those who decreed the rules of conduct without consulting the populace. At least, not her kind of populace. Her kind of populace didn't count, they were not organized, no one was interested in their ill-informed opinions. Ill-informed because everybody knew cigarettes were bad for you, and those who still smoked could safely be shunned and ignored like all other undesirables.

She didn't think of herself as an undesirable, no, she didn't, but did find herself cowering in face of the presumed judgment of those around her. They had more money, more clout, more everything. Or, that was the impression they gave. Maybe deep inside, they cowered just as much as she. There was always someone on top in the social and business stratosphere. Whatever the case, she was a people, too, a real person, a person with a nose to sniff the goings on, a person who could open her mouth and say hello and thank you.

A hint of a thought too vague for words, floated across the opaque slate behind her clear forehead. When she shut her eyes, she saw a straight bright line that went from one end to the other, like the stilled line across the screen of a monitoring machine when the heart stopped beating. Like all machines, it was exact and indifferent, it performed its task as it was supposed to. Henceforth—she thought—I must make changes, small as they may be. So small that even I, the changer and the changed, won't notice them. Since I will be changed —she reasoned further—it stands to reason that I won't notice.

Yes! Again, she motioned the bartender to fill her glass, which he, dutiful and attentive, promptly did. I love you, she wanted to say. I love you for being there, behind the counter, so tall and reassuring, with a quick and honest hand that pulls yet another bill from the pile near my glass. I've come prepared, there's more in my pocket, just in case the pile grows thin and the last bill is suddenly, regretfully, gone.

Outside, the night was young and brilliant; inside, people talked and laughed as they usually do in bars. That was the idea, wasn't it? People gathered together because people needed people. It was in the songs they sang, and in the stories they told. Elections come and go, but the Republic still stands, some pundit said on TV. It was meant to comfort people like her, but it didn't.

She sighed. *Hello and thank you!* And, maybe later, *goodbye*. She was hungry!

If only she could light up and still her hunger. She felt a bit dizzy and too self-conscious to order food and eat it. . . .

Next to her, something was ringing—a cell phone, it turned out. Now its owner was shouting into it, telling the caller where he was, who he was with, and what he was doing. Please don't shout, she wanted to say, but didn't want to antagonize him. No one else thought to complain, so she kept her mouth shut. Hello and thank you. And maybe goodbye. So simple and polite. She was polite, and she was simple. Maybe even simple-minded. Simple never hurt anyone, although it was impossible to tell for sure.

The man had finished giving his report and put his cell phone on the counter. She looked at the small, cute machine. It made her think of a small turtle, and then of a vagina without the slit. Like all machines, it was vibrant, and yet so still. One of its lights—a green one—was blinking, and she wondered why and what it might mean. Probably nothing, just like the weather. She felt a twinge of triumph, welcoming the logic that somehow always threaded her thoughts.

She reached for the small, blinking machine and dropped it between her knees.

It made a soft "click" as it hit the floor, and she flinched, instinctively. No one had heard it but her, and she looked down to see if it was still blinking. She might be lynched, she thought. By the mob. The machine went on blinking, which pleased her. The machine didn't mind where it was, on the counter or on the floor, and she considered it might be time to go home.

"Please, what time is it?" she inquired of the man who had just lost his cell phone. Her eyes rested pensively on his jaw, so set and determined, so sure of its place in the world; a Republican jaw, she mused. The Republic still stood thanks to men like him.

He turned from his friends and looked at her, then pointed at the big round clock above the bottles.

"Oh," she said. "Thank you." And *Hello!*

So, she thought. He would talk to his machine, but not to her. And what about manners? Not to mention chivalry? But, she concluded, he must have his reasons, we all do. She was a mischievous little bitch, and he saw right through her. Didn't even pretend, didn't even make the effort to pretend that she was worth even a moment of his time. Ah, well, to each his own, she thought. She could take a hint, sometimes even two!

The friends of the cell phone man began to discuss locks, and one of them said, shouted really: "If you want security, and you have six locks on your door, you know what to do, right? You make sure you lock only every *other* lock, so when the bad guys come and begin to unlock the locks, they'd be locking three. Get it?"

I get it, she thought. She looked at the diminished pile of bills. Just enough for the tip. She thought of deficits and the national debt as she gathered herself off the stool and walked in a straight line toward the door. She expected a heavy hand to land on her shoulder, but none did. Once I'm out, she thought, no one would miss me. No one would think to think of me. Which, after all was said and done, was all for the good.

She walked home, she knew the way. Up and up the upward-sloping road, then turn right into a side, quiet street. She liked the idea of side and quiet. She liked the idea of keys and locks and homeland security. This was the good life, the life of the city. It hummed its noises, its self-confidence, its ordered red lights. Yes, she was a people, a person, her smallness notwithstanding. Precious blood flowed in her veins, carrying oxygen to vital parts. Plasma and cells. The blood of our nation, someone had said on TV. The sacrifices every one of us has to make.

APPETITES

"Have you noticed how wives snap at their husbands? When guests are present?" Pauline, my friend these past thirty years or so, addressed me as soon as Dolores, her maid, had served the main course and left the room. I was admiring the piece of steamed salmon on my plate, inhaling its delicate aroma and itching to reach for my fork, just when Pauline spoke up. Even though she intoned it as a question, it was really a statement; Pauline, as a rule, solicits a response as mere echo or corroboration of her own proclamations.

"Yes," I said, trying to appear casual as I picked up fork and knife. "I've had occasion to—"

"But," Pauline continued. "Is it the guests who make the wives more irritable than usual, or are the wives just irritable? And why?"

"Maybe," I ventured, "it's the old, you know, familiarity breeds contempt?" I quickly cut a piece of the salmon and put it in my mouth. Pure delight!

"No dear." Pauline finally reached for her fork and knife. "The wives are not getting it, pure and simple. Some things are, you know, simple." Pauline paused to put a small cube of grilled asparagus in her mouth. "You see, their husbands don't excite them anymore, and that's where the famed headaches come in. If the wives had the guts they'd find a lover, but, for the most part, they're passive, they don't do it." Pauline dabbed at her mouth, then placed her white, now lipstick-stained linen napkin back in her lap. "It's sad, very sad."

I nodded, chewing circumspectly. For a time, she remained quiet, cutting into her salmon and chewing, so I was able to eat in peace. Every time Pauline went on like this, about husbands and sex, I thought about that old lady on TV who gave advice to late-night callers, while fondling dildos and vibrators in her age-spotted hands. Pauline and the lady on TV are more or less the same age, I think. Pauline and I don't discuss age, politics, or religion. I've tried many times, in my mind at least, to describe Pauline, her face, that is, since the body, aside from being wide and stocky, is ordinary enough, solid and strong but not fat. She has small dark eyes, like buttons, I guess, but there's a spark in them, I would even say a very lively spark. They're sharp, too, those eyes, and when she gives you a certain look you have to hold her gaze as proof that you are hiding nothing, that you are guile-free.

Let's see. Her nose is kind of prominent, and her skin, well, her skin is not her best feature, it's thick and her pores show. But, she dresses well. Even for our little get-together lunches, she puts on a fresh, pink-ish-orangey dress, with large yellow buttons going down the front. She takes good care of herself and the results, subtle as they may be, are palpable. A man, I imagine, may find her sexually appealing, since, on the whole, she does present a quite attractive package. All a potential suitor need do is consider the milk baths, the perfumed massages, the silky undergarments, to get his mind inflamed. If I were a man, she would have gotten my attention.

Pauline was watching me, and I realized I hadn't responded to her comment about the wives not daring to take on a lover.

"Well, yes, you're right, of course," I said, "but I've heard stories about wives in the suburbs sleeping with the lawn boy, the window washer, the postman, you name it." I put in my two cents, fulfilling my duty as the sole guest.

"Don't tell me you believe such stories." Pauline resumed eating. I forgot to mention that not only was she large, she had large appetites and seemed to revel in them as her given right; this, too, was a point in her favor. She ate slowly, daintily, savoring every bite. I had already finished my small portion (smaller than hers, I believe) and was now sipping my second chilled chardonnay.

"Well," I said, conceding that maybe I didn't believe such stories, either. "But!" I suddenly remembered. "I have a friend, right here in the city, who took the supermarket delivery boy to her bed. I know this for a fact since she told me so herself."

Pauline gave me a look with those sharp little eyes, and for a moment I thought that she thought it was I who had taken the boy to my bed.

"Pathetic, though, isn't it?" Pauline said, putting a morsel of steamed salmon in her mouth.

"Yes, but she needed it, and so she did it. He was handsome, she said, and had very smooth skin. I don't see anything wrong with a woman taking a young guy to bed."

"Neither do I. I just think it's pathetic, that's all."

I shrugged, fiddling with the heavy silver fork on the white tablecloth. "I read an article about a few men in a slaughterhouse carving holes in the side of a cow and raping her, so to speak, in the holes. Not one of them, incidentally, used the one, or two actually, real holes, which I found strange."

Pauline nearly gagged. "Is *that* what you find strange? The whole thing is sick, horridly and morally sick. Where did you hear such a story?"

"That was my point, precisely. Women may resort to pathetic solutions once in a while, but men . . ."

"I see." Pauline heaved her bosom. She had finished eating and pushed her plate aside. As if on cue, Dolores arrived and cleared the table in her customary efficient and quiet manner. I normally feel ill at ease when I'm being served, even in restaurants, but with Dolores, I don't know, it doesn't bother me one bit. I have to say, I love coming here, to Pauline's, for lunch or dinner. The food is always superb, and thanks to Dolores neither of us need to lift a finger. This is a luxury I don't enjoy at home.

As we sat and waited for the dessert— my favorite course—I let my mind wander, trying to imagine what kind of dessert Dolores would bring to the table. Last time I was here, two months or so ago, Dolores served the most delicate flourless chocolate cake, with a small mound of whipped cream and crushed nuts on a side plate.

"As gruesome as your story is," Pauline spoke up, "men have a long, you know . . ." She smiled mysteriously as I held my breath. ". . . history, doing it with animals, usually sheep. Fitting." Pauline smacked her lips, and a sudden laugh burst out of me.

"You're funny," I said, knowing she liked to be told she was funny.

"They like to do things together, like in a team, you know? Especially when they rape something or someone. These are the normal ones among them, those who also like to masturbate together. Then, of course, you have the real psychos, the killers and the serial killers. They don't only rape you, they kill you, too, and sometimes dine on preferred body parts. God knows what goes on in the heads of such, well, what should I call them, they don't belong in the human race, obviously, they're animals, worse than animals, uncivilized, barbaric creatures."

I nodded, thinking that animals, mostly, are gentle, and vegetarian, animals like cows and horses, but I knew what she meant, so I just said, "I know what you mean."

"Maybe they didn't go for the real holes because those would have been harder to reach? You'd need to climb a stool or something," Pauline said.

I glanced toward the kitchen, motioning to Pauline that Dolores could hear our vile conversation. Pauline had a strong, authoritative voice, she wasn't one to whisper.

Pauline dismissed my concern with a wave of her hand. "Nothing she hasn't heard before. Don't forget where she comes from."

"Of course."

Dolores came from Honduras and, according to the stories she had told Pauline over the years, had seen every type of brutality imaginable, toward man and beast alike. We were very fortunate, Pauline had said more than once, to have had the privilege to grow up and live in a country like the U.S.

Dolores entered, pushing a cart, and we both straightened up in our chairs. We smiled, our hands in our laps. Dolores poured our coffee into small china cups, and then placed the most delectable-looking banana cream pie on our dessert plates.

"My favorite," Pauline exclaimed, and I nodded excitely; it was my favorite, too. "Isn't she wonderful?" Pauline said, briefly placing her ringed hand on Dolores's arm. "She always surprises me. What would I have done without her?"

Dolores smiled, then retreated discreetly to the kitchen. I wondered, not for the first time, if she was allowed to partake of the same food as her mistress and her guests.

We picked up our spoons and dipped into the pies.

"Scrumptious," I said, filled with gratitude to Pauline, to Dolores, to my good fortune. Then, strangely, inexplicably, an emptiness filled me, a kind of anxiety I guess, and I remembered my mother, nearly ninety, in a nursing home up in Yonkers. I go to see her once a month, and during my last visit the whole place was under extreme scrutiny as it was alleged, by a visiting family member, a lawyer no less, that a nurse, a female, had made sexual use of his father, an old man who was half comatose. He had caught her in the act, the lawyer said. I was trying to decide if this was a story I wanted to share with Pauline, when Pauline suddenly put down her spoon and said, "Any mention of the cow's tits?"

"The cow's tits?" I repeated, looking at her as if she'd flipped. It took a couple of seconds before I understood what she was referring to. "No, no mention of the tits."

"I find *that* curious." Pauline picked up her spoon.

"Yeah, me too."

We ate our banana cream pies, and sipped our coffees.

"You'd think, you know, that men would go after the tits," Pauline said. "If only as foreplay."

"With a cow?"

"Well, yes. If a cow, as sexual target, strikes your fancy."

This was quite funny, I thought, but I had just put a spoonful of banana cream in my mouth and couldn't laugh, so I pressed one hand to my lips and sent the other aflutter, indicating that I thought her remark was very funny.

"Maybe they did go after the tits, but the man who told the story forgot to mention it?" I said once I'd swallowed.

"Strange. People are strange," Pauline said dreamily, scratching her left nostril with the nail of her pinky. "We live in a strange world, strange times. Life is not what it used to be."

Pauline paused, and I opened my mouth, prepared to announce that truer words were never said, but she continued. "Even a small thing as a sponge, so Dolores informs me, is not what it used to be. It used to be that you paid, I don't know, a buck for a dozen good sponges that would last you a lifetime, but these days you buy two for $1.99, and they crumble in your hands in no time at all. Ah, well, life continues."

"Sponges, yes, I know," I said. I was beginning to feel drowsy, which usually happens after dessert; that's one of the peculiar drawbacks to a rich and satisfying lunch. I looked forward to getting into a cab, then riding home through the park, arriving at my building where Tony, the doorman, would pull the door and greet me as if he were truly happy to see me, and I'd go up the elevator and into my hushed, dim apartment and, after a short stop in the bathroom, would get into my bed and take a little nap.

COUNT YOUR BLESSINGS

The ladies sat on thin-legged chairs on the lawn. They were served drinks, and they drank. The groomed butler was the lover of two of them. He was ambitious—two more had made it into his modest but promising list, both marked in light pencil, for he had yet to confirm their intentions. The ladies chatted, oblivious. It was warm, their drinks were cool and refreshing. Their insides tingled. The tree above, like a benevolent father, sent down its arms in a shading embrace. Even so, a few of them, mindful of their exquisitely maintained pale skin, made use of individual fringed parasols, which sprouted above their heads in yellows and pinks.

They couldn't complain, they agreed, life was good. If not always good, then at least always comfy. And, when not absolutely comfy, there were benefits and compensations in one form or another. In short, life placed no unreasonable demands on them, as, for example, the chairs that supported the bones of their delicate behinds. Admittedly, the chairs were not comfortable *per se*, but they were of a style and a design that granted the ladies and their spines a light and airy elegance; in fact, they seemed to be floating or hovering rather than sitting. The chairs had been pre-arranged (by the butler) in a circle, or an oval, so that the ladies could see and hear each other when they spoke. And the butler, since he was there, refreshing their drinks, listened as well. Now and again, he feigned a reserved smile, usually when bending down and deferentially lighting a cigarette for one of his lovers, or for a potential one. He was ambitious, yes, but also generous. He thought women were a scream. Especially these women with their funny little parasols, seated in a circle and chattering at leisure, very much like birds in a tree.

"Are you ready for the snacks?" the butler thought to ask Mrs. C., the lady of the house.

Mrs. C. lingered. She appeared to be considering the butler's question, but in truth was a bit distressed by his use of "snacks." Not terribly distressed, but distressed enough to feel as though a tiny insect were disturbing the air near her nose.

"Are we ready for little scrumptious things?" she asked, turning over the decision-making to the ladies.

The ladies couldn't or wouldn't say.

"Mmmmm," said Mrs. T.

"Well, maybe. . . ." said Mrs. L.

"Oh, snacks?" said Mrs. V., dreamily looking up at the butler and smiling.

The butler's insides tingled. So much beauty and so little time! And dear Mrs. V. She'd never paid him any mind, and here she was, under the tree, part of a circle, smiling up at him, and so sweetly, too. Of course he understood that her smile meant little—these ladies smiled often and obliquely—but still, she must have been aware, even dimly, that he was only the butler, and yet she smiled.

Mrs. C. sighed. "Well, yes, I guess we're ready," she addressed the butler without looking at him.

"Very well, madam." The butler gave a little bow and hurried toward the side entrance of the house. In the kitchen, young Loretta was still fussing over the little scrumptious things. Once in a while, she licked her fingers, then wiped them on her apron.

"Take your time," the butler told her. "They're not very hungry."

"Hungry!" Loretta snorted. "You must be joking."

"Well," the butler said. He and Loretta shared a bed every now and then, and they understood one another. He popped a piece of lobster into his mouth, then stood by the open window and lit a cigarette.

Watching the ladies from afar, he suddenly felt very protective of them, very much as if he were the shepherd and they his helpless lambs, strewn about on a lawn under a Quaking Aspen tree.

"Life is good," he announced.

"Bah!"

"I know." The butler laughed and took a long drag. The ladies, he realized, were looking toward the house, maybe longing for him. Once in a while, a hand rose and moved a hair, or scratched a nose, lightly.

"How long have you had him?" Mrs. T. asked Mrs. C.

"Had him?" Mrs. C. seemed startled.

"The butler," Mrs. T. explained.

"Oh, the butler." Mrs. C. turned pensive. "About three months, I think."

"Mmmm. Where did you find him?" Mrs. V. joined the conversation.

Smiling, Mrs. C. turned to Mrs. V. "I don't quite remember, frankly, but he came highly recommended."

"No doubt," said Mrs. V.

"He is very fluid," the ladies murmured their unanimous assent. "Very silent. Professional."

"Yes, we're blessed." Mrs. C. sniffed modestly. An image she wasn't prepared for floated behind her clear forehead, and she shuddered.

"Are you all right?" Mrs. V. inquired, leaning forward, reaching a slender arm toward her friend.

"Yes, quite. I think I may be hungry, after all."

"Me, too." Mrs. L. giggled.

Mrs. C. looked toward the house. She considered picking up the remote control from the side table and buzzing the butler, but didn't want to appear impatient, or worse, give the impression that her butler's timing was off. So far, the outing had been a success and just as idyllic as planned; none of the ladies seemed to notice that the butler was dawdling in the kitchen. Of course, she knew what he was doing, taking liberties and smoking a cigarette by the window, while chatting with Loretta. Mrs. C. resolved not to bother.

"I love pain-killers," Mrs. L. murmured.

"Pain-killers, yes," Mrs. T. said. "You have a pain, you take a little pill and poof! it's gone. Genius."

Mrs. V. laughed. "Marvelous, yes! A kind of miracle, really. Myself, I love a good shower-head."

"Moi aussi!" Mrs. Z. suddenly piped up, surprising Mrs. C. Mrs. C. had noticed how Mrs. Z. had been eyeing the butler—like a hawk. Mrs. Z. wasn't French, but she liked to use the French language when opportunity arose.

"Really?" Mrs. C. said, staying just on this side of nasty. "I thought you only took baths."

Mrs. Z. eyed Mrs. C. What's got into her? she wondered. It was unlike Mrs. C. to be so confrontational. "Well, I do both, you know, I take a bath, and then I shower. I love the way water feels on my skin."

"Why, yes, of course." Mrs. C. smiled to break the thin layer of ice that began to form around the circle. She ached to glance at her watch. She had a massage at two, she had to be rid of her guests by a quarter to, and still her butler was nowhere in sight—what was she to do? Sometimes life was just too overwhelming, too frustrating. A minute longer, she knew, and she'd burst into tears.

Mrs. C. stood up. "The little girls' room." She laughed and waved and turned toward the house. She walked slowly, as if taking pleasure in every step, yet her heart raced madly ahead, but also backward, wondering if the ladies were discussing her and what they were saying now that her back was turned. Was she going insane? She could feel how every precious drop of reason was deserting her. She wasn't a bad person, why did such annoying things have to happen to her? She only meant well, why couldn't the world conform to her wishes? The truth was, she was hypersensitive, she took everything to heart, and she had such a large heart. She should learn to be more aloof, less caring. Even Mr. C.—not the most perceptive man in the world—had said this about her, so there!

Mrs. C. felt her lips moving. It was silly, of course, but talking to herself like this made her feel better, calmer. There was still the issue of the butler to be taken up and dealt with, but now she had gathered the necessary fortitude to face him. She had made one mistake with him, never to be repeated. She was weak then, but was strong now. Women around menopause time were known to be fragile, volatile, and she was no exception.

She entered the house and turned right, toward the kitchen, calling: "Loretta!" in that special tone she reserved for servants. It was a tone naked of pretense and sure of itself, sure of its commands. Indeed, it should surprise no one that Mrs. C. expected Loretta to come running out of the kitchen, but no one came running out of the kitchen.

This is just too much! Mrs. C. thought, panic rising in her as she marched resolutely into the kitchen. She couldn't believe her eyes. Empty! No butler, no Loretta! Probably having their afternoon nookie somewhere in the house. Her house! She'll fire them both on the spot!

"I'm here, ma'am." Loretta came rushing, wiping her hands on her apron. "I was in the washroom."

"Oh." Mrs. C. looked around her, then fixed her gaze on the large, rectangular table. "Where's the food?"

Loretta seemed confused. "The butler took it," she said, pointing toward the lawn.

"Oh." Now it was Mrs. C. who seemed confused. She walked to the window and, indeed, saw the butler bowing politely as he served her guests. What *is* the matter with her? Why is she *always* so quick to blame and find fault?

Relieved and grateful and summoning her dignity, Mrs. C. smiled at Loretta. "You're right, of course. Yes," she said and walked out to the lawn. She took her seat and reached for a little scrumptious thing from the tray the butler held before her. Everything was just perfect. The weather, the drinks, the little scrumptious things, even the butler, not to mention Loretta who laid it out oh so tastefully. The ladies seemed happy, chewing and sipping. And only two minutes ago, how silly she was, so fearful, as a kitten, ready to give in, to collapse mentally and physically and ask to be sent to a sanatorium. What a soothing name for a place where one could rest and convalesce. It probably came from the Latin, and she had studied some Latin once, so very long ago. *Morituri te salutant*, popped into her head.

"Livi, this is just too deliciously lovely," Mrs. T. squeaked. "I've always maintained you were the best. You have the best of all Midas touch."

"Thank you *so* much," Mrs. C. said, and meant it. She liked it when people around her voiced their pleasure, especially when she was the source of the pleasure. "The day, indeed, turned out to be super-fine."

"I count my blessings every day," said Mrs. T.

"That's a good thing to do," Mrs. L. said. "Remember to be grateful, and remember to do good."

"Absolutely," the ladies agreed enthusiastically, "what else is there?"

They sipped their drinks, each pretending not to notice the few remaining little scrumptious things on the tray in the butler's hand; it would simply be too impolite and greedy to reach for one. The butler, counting on their good manners, already figured that the last four pieces belonged to him and Loretta, if not by right, then by cultural dicta.

"Of course, there's the war in Iraq," Mrs. Z. suddenly said, speaking softly as if waking from a dream.

The ladies stared at her in disbelief.

"Gosh, you're so *misguided* sometimes," Mrs. V. chided, but gently, as if addressing a clumsy child who stumbled all the time. "Or, so *gauche*, if you prefer."

Mrs. Z. giggled nervously. She knew she had committed a faux pas, and now thought of ways to extricate herself.

She moved a cautious hand over her hairdo. "Frankly, I can't explain it," she said, inviting a tremor into her voice. "You have to understand." She paused. "My son, William, is home for spring break, and that's all he talks about." Mrs. Z. blushed for good measure.

The ladies nodded sympathetically, acknowledging the quandary; they, too, had sons and daughters in college.

Mrs. C., momentarily confounded like her guests, instinctively understood that as hostess it was her implicit duty to take charge of the situation and salvage the afternoon. Her first impulse was to remind the feckless Mrs. Z. to give thanks that the draft had been abolished and that her son was in college and not on some godforsaken battlefield. But, she reconsidered, why waste time on a dead-end topic? A *cul de sac!* Hmm . . . that blasted French again!

Excitedly, she clasped her hands together and called, "Well, I think it's time for dessert," and the ladies agreed that indeed it was time. With a subtle bat of an eye, Mrs. C. gave the butler his marching orders and he, attentive and regimented as ever, nearly clicked his heels and hurried toward the house with his booty.

INTELLIGENT DESIGN OR A NATION OF HARLOTS

Wherefore, O harlot, hear the word of the LORD: Thus saith the Lord GOD; Because thy filthiness was poured out, and thy nakedness discovered through thy whoredoms with thy lovers, and with all the idols of thy abominations . . . Behold, therefore I will gather all thy lovers, with whom thou hast taken pleasure, and all them that thou hast loved, with all them that thou hast hated; I will even gather them round about against thee, and will discover thy nakedness unto them, that they may see all thy nakedness.   Ezekiel 16:35,36, 37

And so the day came when men, in a consensus vote to stop harlotry, put into manifesto and I.D. law that Woman must be forever deprived of male-engendered pleasure. She may secretly engage in self-love, or frolic with her sisters, but when Man engaged in the act, he would give Woman minimum strokes and finish the procreation job just as soon as his penis cooperated.

The women mourned. Not all of them, but enough to cause a dent. Some feared that if left unattended, the dent would become a black hole that would suck in our good earth for an everlasting spin, very possibly a close relation of the legendary Hell.

Hosanna! cried some. Welcome Armageddon! cried others. Give women what's coming to them by birthright! cried a few.

A healthy, if fiery, debate began on many screens and in many tongues, while the tallest building in the universe was being erected in Dubai, which didn't help matters; some speculated that optimum power mass will shift from West to East.

Chaos and general confusion ensued. Polarizing opinion pieces proliferated, tempers flared. Some grumbled, Been there, done that. Exotic men in white robes ran in deserts, wielding infidel firearms and calling for *jihad*. A secret Women's Council—not unlike the mythical Elders of Zion—met every night after supper to decide on a course of action. Here, too, the debate was healthy and fiery.

Let them kill each other, was one general view.

Woman First Man Never, was another. We must save them from themselves, one brave soul said as she stood up to speak, but was soon heckled off the stage.

And yours truly? She stood on the sidelines, seething but passive. She hadn't had sex with a man for quite a while, so the debate, on her side, was purely academic (or, in the words of a famous sister, kakademic). She did raise her hand, however, and went on stage one night—after a superior supper of soft-shell crabs—and suggested, with surprising vibrancy: O harlots, hold your horses! A dent is a dent is a dent, and the black hole, one of many. Look around the room, for Pete's sake, and take the bull by its horns!

So they did! They looked around the room, went home to their mates, a smack or two were dealt, Man opened his eyes and abundant light poured in and poured out.

COMBO-SUITE

1. Livers

She was on a crusade to save his liver. He said, Careful there with
CRUSADE—
remember what's his face? Bush?
Later he said: Don't worry about my liver, there's more of me, you know,
go for other parts, touch me here, there.
So she did. She touched him here, there.
Most often, it felt good to touch the parts he pointed to.
Sometimes some parts revolted and shrank.
She shrank, too, feeling inadequate and lacking, even though he kept
insisting that it wasn't her, it was him, something to do with enlarged
prostates and shrinking libidos.

And so, she concentrated on other parts of his immense body.
Usually, the middle of it, which was hard "as a rock."
Hallelujah!—she chanted.
Ditto!—he echoed.
God Bless America!—they chanted together while watching baseball.

2. Ankles

When she wasn't with *him*, she walked the streets, dreaming of trans-
atlantic flights. Such *grandeur!* She saw Paris, she saw Berlin, but most
often she saw London, so in-the-news lately. I'll go out there and hook

up with Banksy, she thought, or that soccer person whose name she happened to forget—how could she?—but whose name, she recalled, also began with a B. The guy himself, she also knew (being up-to-date on the news), was on his way to New York and already complaining of swollen ankles. It's always something, she thought unhappily. Livers, ankles, prostates; it always rains on us, women.

3. (After) Two Serious Ladies

One day she bumped into Bernice, an elegant woman she knew from the neighborhood, a famous oddball, who more or less proposed to her, right there on the street, near the lovely park on First Avenue and Seventeenth Street. (Later, she told *him* about this, verbatim.)

"Hello Rolanda, may I ask you something?" Bernice asked, stumbling a bit, all confused and shy, and she (named Rolanda, obviously), already charmed, said, "Why, of course," all so innocent and tickled.

"Yes, yes," said Bernice, "will you come home with me? It's not very far, you'll like it, you'll have your own bed, a room of your own, until we part."

"Part? Part where?" Rolanda asked, still innocent and tickled, while the dear lady Bernice was wringing her elegant hands, and Rolanda's heart, too.

"Listen," said Rolanda, "stop this wringing. It hurts," and Bernice stopped, giving Rolanda a certain look through her stylish shades and letting out a feeble sigh.

"Yes, you're right, it's a revolting habit, forgive me. Will you come?"

"Yes, why not, hand in hand to the Eiffel Tower, okay?"

"Okay," said Bernice, "and maybe also a trip to the Sunshine State?"

"Fine with me," said Rolanda, and the two proceeded, uncertainly, into a trompe-l'oeil depicting tranquility.

BLISS

She is in love again. She runs home after work to do the laundry, cook dinner for the two of them. She's always out of breath, intoxicated; she must be drunk with success, her sense of accomplishment.

She calls me on the telephone to complain. "I neglect my friends," she says. "I don't seem to have time for anything anymore."

I listen, straining to catch that particular quiver in her voice that will betray the real reason for her call. Sartre called it "mauvaise foi." She doesn't speak French, but she must know she is now engaged in self-congratulation rather than true regret.

I decide to be generous. I tell her to enjoy it while it lasts; these are difficult times.

"But you don't understand," she continues. "I don't have my life to myself anymore."

I can't wait to hang up. Who does she think she is kidding? Their love-making, she says, is great. She gets a healthy dose every morning and every night. This is during the week. On the weekends they also have the afternoons. Life is slow and easy on weekend afternoons.

I'm sprawled on my armchair, looking out the window. I have my weekends, too.

"Where is he now?" I ask. I met him a couple of times, but somehow never manage to remember his name. He is usually quiet and seems to be in a state of shock. His eyes are cloudy, and he doesn't move much. Sometimes, as she describes him, I see him strip off his clothes, slowly, like a somnambulist. Or maybe I am the somnambulist.

"Where is he now?" I ask, and she says, "Here."

"You mean, he can hear every word you say?"

"Why not?" she counters in her high, declamatory voice. "We tell each other everything."

I nod, reflecting that I never allow myself such freedoms, let alone with men. "Do we know what we want?" I say into the phone.

"What do you mean?" she asks.

"Just that. I'm not sure we know what we want." I rise from the chair and look down on the street. It looks lively down there. It's Sunday afternoon, people go in and out of the supermarket, preparing for the week ahead.

"I don't know what you mean," she says. "I know exactly what I want."

"Well, what do you want?"

"I don't like your tone of voice."

"Neither do I," I admit.

"What's wrong?" she demands.

A couple of weeks later we meet for lunch. She looks fabulous. She radiates good health and happiness.

"You look fantastic," I tell her.

"Thanks," she says and hugs me. "It's love," she whispers in my ear.

"Sex," I say.

She orders fruit salad, I order a chili-burger with fries. She plunges right in, tells me more details about their life together, about his never-failing sexual drive. As I watch her lips, my eyes begin to burn, which usually happens when I try too hard to focus and listen, when, in truth, I don't want to listen at all.

Our food arrives, and I attack my burger. She picks at her salad, moves a strawberry back and forth with the obvious luxury of one for whom food is no longer important. Soon, she'll offer me the fruit remaining on her plate, but I won't touch it. The vivid positions of their love-making, the uses she makes of her mouth and hands, too readily spring to mind.

The strawberry finally lands in her mouth, and now her mouth is full of juices.

"You're quiet," she says after she swallows.

"You're the one with the news," I say, trying to sound friendly and neutral.

"Are you jealous?" she asks.

"Of what?" *How dare she?*

"Forget it," she says.

"No. Why should I be jealous?"

"Because."

She doesn't let go, does she? In the name of absolute honesty, she doesn't let go. I call the waitress and ask for a glass of water. I am furious, but am determined to finish my lunch; I, too, have rights.

She is pale now. "I didn't mean to upset you," she says.

"It's all right."

"I know I'm full of it," she continues, "but I can't help myself. Is this bliss or what?"

I smile, nodding. Well, yes, she is the friend I know, after all. "Must be."

I drink my water and observe her narrow lips float at the bottom of my glass. I think ahead to a time, perhaps six months, perhaps a year, when they will no longer be together, and I will tire of consoling her, but will do it all the same.

NOT LIKE THIS

They've had a rough night, but now, sitting on their balcony with their morning coffee—she in a dark blue dress, pink flip-flops, sunglasses, rollers on her head; he in a black, short-sleeved shirt, red shorts—they seem poised, composed. God only knows what's in her head as he talks, raising his hand toward the horizon. We don't know what's in her head, but she sits up straight, holding her mug with both hands. The mugs, it so happens, are white, and so are the hands.

She may be thinking about yesterday, about her awful experience, calling her insurance company, and then sitting and listening for about 30 minutes to the charmingly pleasant male voice that kept whispering in her ear: *Please hold while we're transferring you to an account specialist, the expected wait time is 14 minutes, meanwhile, may we offer you more services from our basket of excellence?*

At first she held on, as if mesmerized, but in the end she broke down and sobbed and screamed at her husband, Why is this happening to me? To his credit, he took it like a man; he was calm, and he tried to calm her. She was a good woman. She was clean and often domestic in the traditional ways. She made sure their closets smelled nice, that the silver and glassware shone when she raised them to the light. She tried to remember when and how she became so obsessively clean, but couldn't. Maybe she'd always been clean, but never thought to think or worry about it.

Maybe her erstwhile lover popped into head, erstwhile, mind you, only since yesterday. Everything went wrong yesterday. She had sent him an email, as she had done many times these past few months, but this time he—or, more exactly, the automated program, as she soon realized—responded in a flash, telling her that it had given up, and that the remote host had said about her: *does not like recipient.*

It hurt. It astonished her. Just like that she had been cast aside, no longer the beloved she used to be. Now she could admit to herself, or had to admit to herself, that she had known all along that the relationship would not last forever; that one day, like all things, it would have to end, but not like this, her heart moaned, not like this. And, to make it worse, there was no one she could commiserate with, it was too humiliating, she had to keep her mouth shut and watch her husband's knobby knees as he sat there in his red shorts and pointed at the horizon. The horizon! What did she care about the horizon? The remote host, like any automaton, was heartless, but Bud, her wonderful lover, must have known that such a blunt *does not like recipient* would kill her. Right before the insurance business, she tried to call him, there was so much she needed to say to him, it was all so clear in her head, the words were ready on her lips, Bud, Dearie, where are you? What happened? Only yesterday, both you and your remote host liked me well, always responsive and gracious and loving, and now this. She tried to call, her speech ready, but his answering device cut her off. She tried his Facebook page, but there, too, she was shunned, having lost all Friend privileges.

Her husband rose, shook out his legs and looked at his watch. Really, she thought, he mustn't wear shorts. She considered telling him that, but to what end? The knees were his knees, the rollers were her rollers, night after night the two of them snored together in the same bed— what more did she want?

POST-OP

Post-op she is laid out on a white pillowed bed, so pure, says the nurse, so virgin-like, maybe a corpse, though breathing.

The patient lies between them. Like a shroud, she wants to add, but what's the point?

She knows there are two of them, two nurses, hovering over her bed ... like angels?

She wonders why they discuss her like this, possibly aware that she is awake.

Even her feces, the nurse whispers. So delicate, so beige-like, like a puppy's, or a newborn.

Hallelujah! The patient thinks. Nearly good enough to eat.

FAST LANE

So, you write short shorts. You blog. You used to write novels, not for a living, but for a writing. You gather the reserves of enthusiasm still allowed you, and you tell yourself and others: You'd be surprised how much you can say in 300 words, even 200 words, maybe 50 words. I'm sure you can recall instances when one word was enough, when one word was too much!

Your friends look at you and nod, a nod you've come to suspect and resent, but a nod you yourself are capable of when they talk. You're not exactly on the fast lane, nor on the jet set, and people, even friends, can afford to ignore you. You glimpse the lane and the jet set on television, and your heart contracts with bitter envy, the same heart that knows you are exactly where you belong.

SUITCASES

She married him, in part, for his last name. It had an associative flare and, unlike hers, was solidly American and middle-class.

Often, in the middle of the night, to put things in order, or, possibly, in order to calm her, he opened the fridge and offered her slices of American cheese, which she gratefully slurped down.

"You're a man who knows his bitch," she said, as Bonbon, their 8-year-old terrier, sprawled herself across the brown linoleum floor.

"You're too true to be good," she said further as he patted her sleepy head.

"True-true," he said. "True-true."

NEIGHBORS

She had a strange neighbor of an indeterminate age. He could be twenty, she thought, or maybe forty or fifty. She was new in the building, she had moved in a few months before, full of fresh hopes, hopes that seemed to have materialized, except for this one neighbor who became a blot on her anticipated existence. He had a small baby face, and a slight, stooping frame that gave the impression he was short and deformed, although he wasn't really. She imagined that he had acquired the stoop already as a child, trying to hide, and she felt a sympathy she wanted but could not express. The worst part was his hair, kind of mousy brown, nearly reaching his shoulders, but not quite, for it curled upward in messy clumps. He was always neatly dressed, and was always alone when she saw him, just like she was. She realized that, just as she thought him odd, he probably thought her odd, for she was as alone as he was. She considered, with some discomfort, that if the tenants in the building thought him odd, they probably lumped her with him, in the same category, even if she, unlike the neighbor, was quite attractive, which should indicate, she hoped, that if she was alone, it was definitely by choice. The neighbor, too, she reasoned, should surmise this about her, unless, of course, he didn't have a sense of himself as being peculiar or unappealing. Possibly, when he looked in the mirror he saw a familiar, attractive face, just as she did when she watched herself reflected in the mirror.

Maybe, she thought, she should introduce herself to him and so break the spell, but he never gave her an opening, and so, every time she saw him, she tensed up, and he did, too, as their antennae recognized this thing in one another, this "aloneness," this "oddness," not least because they seemed to keep the same schedule, they bumped into each other too often, mostly in the elevator, each time a bit surprised, giving a start, and then, forlorn and quiet, waiting for the doors to mercifully open so he, who lived a couple of floors below hers, would exit, and both of them would breathe again, released to their natural state.

SHLUG DA KLEINE

One of my very first memories, and one that comes back to me every so often, is of my sister pushing me onto the road and nearly under the hooves of a horse. She was about four years old at the time, and I was five. I don't know how she managed it, I was taller and probably stronger—she was a scrawny little thing with large ears—so I assume she pushed me with all the vehemence a four-year-old can muster.

It's hard to tell who resented whom more, but I'm fairly certain that I never pushed her, and that I never tried to harm her physically. My resentment was purer and more abstract, having to do with fairness and justice. After all, she had arrived thirteen months after I did, she took my crib, and the little creature I called sister showed no respect for me, the one who came before her.

But I also know that I was not an innocent bystander, and it could very well have been anger, rather than deep resentment, that made her push me. Defending my own turf, I saw her as a nuisance and was probably in the habit of belittling her, so it is entirely possible I had said something right before she pushed me. We were standing at the curb, my mother, my sister and I, waiting for my father. Something in me tells me that my sister, usually passive and quiet until provoked, was standing near my mother, and that I, claiming precedence, tried to take her place at my mother's side, and that she, negating that birthright and claiming her own, pushed me onto the road in retaliation.

Still, it is also fair to say that she was born with an attitude, and she often astonished me—and my parents—in her sudden outbursts. When she was barely eight years old she screamed at them, declaring that she did not ask to be born, and since they chose to bring her into the world, they owed her the dress or whatever else she demanded from them. It was such an amazing and novel claim, I remember looking at her with a new awareness, an awareness that made me admire her, if only for a split second, and also envy her, as I asked myself how she, the little one, had come up with such an argument.

Let me pause here a minute. Born with an attitude? Maybe, just as plausibly, she felt she had to fight for her dignity? My father and mother, more than once, talked about my sister having been the result of an unexpected and an unwanted pregnancy. They talked about how difficult it was for my mother to carry her in her belly on the long and torturous journey from Czechoslovakia to Israel. In addition, my sister's large ears were a source of merriment and family jokes, and my father, quite often, liked to repeat the funny story about how I ran to him every evening when he returned from work with the plea: *Shlug da kleine!*

It is also true that my parents, unwittingly, encouraged my belittling of my sister. In their innocent and affectionate bantering about her, they gave me license to do the same, and running up to my father and telling him to beat up my sister was yet another way to make them laugh and ingratiate myself; I was the smart daughter, she was the little monkey I could safely tease.

So, no, I don't know that my sister was born with an attitude, but I do know that she was born with a sweet and generous nature, even if I came to recognize this only years later. In our childhood photographs, large ears and all, she looks like a delicate fragile angel, and her sweet demeanor shines through her pale skin, her large brown eyes. She looks straight at the camera but she rarely smiles, maybe because I'm right next to her, smiling my cocky smile. I had her in my power, or so I believed, when she ran with me in the streets of Jaffa, always silent and always behind—my shadow and in my shadow.

How my parents allowed us to roam the exotic and potentially dangerous streets of Jaffa in the 1950s, I don't know. In many ways, they were laissez-faire parents, perhaps because they both came from very large families where the older child takes charge of the younger ones, while the mother is busy in the kitchen, or gossiping with the neighbors. I don't remember my mother gossiping too often with them, but I do remember her in the kitchen, cooking and baking, bringing to the table delicious meals and desserts made from scratch. I remember breakfasts in particular, my mother asking my sister and me what we want, then placing the plates before us. I gobble down my food, while my sister rejects what she has just asked for and demands—and gets—a different dish.

Another vivid and recurring memory is of the two of us, two years or so later, waiting for the bus to our elementary school. When I saw the bus coming, I told my sister, who was standing on the street, to join me on the sidewalk, which she did, and then, calmly and deliberately, shoved her breakfast slice of bread in my face, smearing me with butter and jam. She then climbed onto the bus, and I climbed in after her, still horrified, humiliated and shocked, mostly because there were people at the station who witnessed my shame and bewilderment. One of them gave me a handkerchief to wipe my face and, if I remember correctly, chided my sister for doing such a terrible thing.

And yet, the same sister who pushed me, who smeared my face with her jam sandwich, and who frequently threw tantrums, is also the sister who massaged my mother's feet when she was ailing and dying. The sister who nursed my father when he was ailing and dying. She is the sister who knew how to make my mother laugh, and who makes me laugh when I visit. She was always more blunt and direct than me, sometimes even brutal, not only toward me and my parents, but toward other people as well, and to this day I find it hard to even begin to disentangle the multitude of nerve-endings and make sense of how I feel about her, or what I feel for her, not only as a sister, but as a person.

She was an indifferent student, never finished high school, and I know that she is aware that her blunt and often petty gossipy remarks annoy me. But she doesn't know, I don't think, that her attempts to impress me sometimes with a book she read or a concert she went to, bring back the memory of the sibling who felt, from the very beginning, that she was the lesser member of the family, and this, quite simply, breaks my heart.

It would be easy for me to say that yes, surely, I love her, I've always loved her, but love seems too small a word and imprecise. At bad moments, when I look for ways to torture myself, I imagine her dead or dying, as if preparing for the devastation should something happen to her. Such attempts last only a millisecond, and my terror is so great, I have to stop.

Every piece of writing is a groping into that foggy and confused place where jumbles of thoughts, memories, and feelings agitate. But this particular jumble, the jumble of sisterhood, is the hardest, as it grows foggier and more suspect with the years. A jumble that only a sibling, who was there much of the way, can help me unravel. A sibling who is now the only chronicler and witness of me as a child. A sibling who remembers me from her own perspective, who watched and saw me from different angles. A sibling I still pit myself against, hoping to get a clearer image of who I was and have become, even if I often don't like what I see.

I feel particularly humbled when I recall the sibling who willingly served as my appointed and loyal spy when, as an adolescent, I went to dance parties and took her along, so she would spy on the boys and later report to me who had eyed me or seemed interested in me, as if it were understood that I was the center of attention, and that no one would be interested in her, my little sister.

A few months after the horse episode, my parents packed us up and we moved into a three-room apartment in a new housing complex for immigrants. We left Jaffa behind and forgot about the room overlooking the sea. We now had to go to a special preschool to learn to speak a new language, Hebrew. On the first day, just before we went in, I took my sister by the hand and, for the first time as I remember it, treated her the way an older and responsible sister is supposed to treat a younger sibling. I told her that we must forget Yiddish and learn to speak Hebrew; this was something that both she and I would have to endure and overcome. I remember the urgency with which I spoke the words, and perhaps that is why, this time, she didn't rebel but listened, serious and quiet. And then, still hand in hand, we walked in.

Except for periodic eruptions throughout our childhood and adolescence, I tolerated my sister following me around and joining me and my friends in our games, and, at my parents' urging, I reluctantly helped her with her homework. There was too much tension between us to ever experience true joy together. This tension is still there, but we've learned to be cautious, something our volatile and bewildered parents couldn't teach us. We've learned to tiptoe around our shortcomings and our differences, but in my dreams, usually involving my mother as well, we have ferocious fights, with me raging against my sister's apparent indifference and thoughtlessness.

There is so much to tell, and it is the nature of memory that bad experiences readily appear in one's psyche where shame and pain are intertwined. When we talk about the past, my sister doesn't recall the incidents about the horse and the jam, nor does she recall the details of more recent confrontations. One of her fondest memories, she says, is the ease with which I studied for my exams: one foot on a chair, the book on the table, and me flipping through the pages. And even though this description amuses and pleases me, I'm also somewhat annoyed that she remains unaware of the times she hurt me and our parents, and maybe that's why I still rage against her, impotently, in my dreams.

My sister and I are middle-aged now and live thousands of miles apart. We talk on the phone, we email. I call her Pieteke, she calls me Sheifale, our father's nicknames for us. She is one of my very few emotional ties to the country I left years ago. She is the flesh and blood link to my dead parents, to a time when the four of us lived in one room and the only luxury we could boast about was the Mediterranean Sea, right outside our window. Through her I'm tethered to something solid and elemental, to a feeling akin to generosity and twinness.

Today would have been my mother's 92nd birthday. One of the enduring family myths is that I was my mother's favorite, and my sister, my father's. It was often said that I took after my mother, and that my sister took after my father. With the years, though, my sister and I look more and more alike, and people easily identify us as sisters. Sometimes I see my father in her, sometimes my mother, just as I see my parents in me. Maybe a day will come and I will recognize myself in my sister, a sister who, on the whole, is humble, good-hearted, and well-meaning.

Often, I reach into the jumble and try to realign it; still, the jumble remains intact, as perhaps it must. And as I reach for reasons and excuses and definitive answers, I become paralyzed. Anecdotes are not the real or the only story, but anecdotes are what we cling to. I had planned to write a nice fictional account about two sisters, but the little one, the one I begged my father to beat up, wouldn't let me.